# Seven Ways To Jane

# Seven Ways To Jane

*M.J. Sewall*

# Contents

*To Junell,*
*I cannot thank you enough for your love, help and*
*support through many adventures.*

# Chapter 1

# The Idea

"You are not who you think you are." - Silvia
Hartmann

*Was everything a lie? All these other Jane Waldens,
what the hell was that for? To teach me a lesson? Great.
Got it Fate, thanks. But, did you have to take everything? I mean, what has it been, ten days on the road?
Less than that? I hold this stupid book in my hand, this
awesome, stunning beautiful book while I wait for my
ridiculously delayed flight at La Guardia.*

*Okay, Fate – I'm over the cliff, my rope is frayed and
I'm spent, and I'm sobbing, and I'm slipping. I have to
know. Show me the connections. What was the actual
link in the chain that started this?*

*Wait... oh yeah, it was that night. That night, and
the liquor ice cream.*

(Fate here - note to Jane: It started exactly eleven days ago...)

"Fired. Sacked. Picture of Todd stuffed into a file box, shown the door. Shit." spewed Jane Walden, pacing her tiny apartment floor.

Christian pushed the glasses up his nose. "Calm down. That's why I brought the Snobar ice cream and bottle of Fireball. Okay, so the lousy PR internship didn't work out. Time to finally write a book. It's your oldest dream."

"Just write a book, he says, my one true friend. Wait..." Jane paced some more. "You said there is also booze *in* the ice cream?"

Christian nodded with a wry smile.

"Genius move, Snobar people." Jane reverted to her tirade. "I'm not even with Todd anymore, but that's the one personal thing that was on my desk. Well, that and the picture of you and me making faces... okay, I'm rambling. Back to your point, my beautiful, brilliant, bespectacled Christian: people who don't write just don't get it. To write, you need an idea first. Sure, you have been super supportive of my writing since High School. I mean, we worked on the school newspaper together...."

"Also, I was an English Lit major, don't forget." Christian reminded.

Jane allowed that. "Yes, but writing a book is a big thing. Where's the idea? The idea, I repeat, while imagining bold curvy neon letters, blinking on and

2

off like every sign outside a film noir hotel room: I need a killer IDEA."

Christian ignored the rising drama, and took a shot of Fireball.

Jane continued, "Yes, I write stunningly amazing prose and kick-ass poetry... that no one reads. Not to mention, my claim-to-zero-fame is as the writer of in-depth piercing exposé of school water polo team in-fighting. Plus, my friend, I've peeked out into the real-world - it's a big, wild, weird, very crowded world of wannabe authors."

"You can do anything." Christian tempered the compliment with her old nickname, "Little Plain Jane just needs a hook. A simple, elegant idea that is at once a plot, a great story foundation, and can be filled with all the dark and interesting machinations of human experience." He shrugged, smiling. "How hard can it be?" Christian swallowed another spoonful of Snobar and decided to sip his shot glass of Fireball. "Okay. Let's think of one. How about your family? They're a little crazy. Some story potential there."

Jane pondered this as she took another shot of Fireball. She laid down across her bed, on her stomach, in the apartment she was about to lose, sans job. Her fingers absently swirled her light brown hair. The cinnamon whiskey gave her a delicious burn as it traveled all the way to her toes. She soothed it with a spoonful of Brandy Alexander Chocolate Chip. She rejected Christian's idea. "Nope. Not crazy enough. I need Blanche Dubois crazy."

"Your sister's crazy enough. Nice mid-century reference, by the way." They clinked shot glasses to celebrate Jane's cleverness. "I'm not sure Blanche from *Streetcar Named Desire* was crazy, exactly. Well, maybe by the end..."

"But my sister's boring crazy. Like everyone-knows-someone-like-her crazy. Besides, If I wrote about her, she'd kill me with her silent, ever-present judgement."

Christian rubbed the back of his neck, his short dark hair neatly rounded at the back. Jane noticed the familiar motion that accompanied his hard thinking. *If he was hot, it would be sexy*, Jane thought. She said, "Don't think too hard, my little Christian Jew. Might start a fire up there in your noggin."

"That old wildly racist nickname again? Okay, *Plain Jane* – if we really are reviving the old monikers we gave each other. Also, watch it - you know I'm smarter than you." he said, "Besides, I've told you Jacobson is not a Jewish surname, remember?"

She shrugged and took another shot. "I'm forced to reminisce back over our twenty-three years, after my recent financial reversals. How long have we known each other, anyway?"

"Eleven. We were eleven-year-olds when we met. Me in the giant thick glasses and you in the Laura Ingalls-inspired floral dress."

Jane laughed, "Oh my God, I remember that. Two ready-made victims for sixth grade bullying."

"You were the only one who would talk to me." Christian smiled. "I think the teachers were embar-

4

rassed for us." He chased the ice cream with the rest of his shot. "This ice cream is really good."

"Heck yah, it is. Did they have other flavors?"

"Yes. But tonight called for chocolate," he said, pushing the glasses up on his nose. "Jane, the real problem is, you don't really know yourself."

That made Jane pause. "Wait, me? I know myself... hey, I got the job I wanted."

"Correction, you got the internship for the job you kinda-sorta wanted – the one you wanted only after panicking Junior year and changing your major. A nice paid PR internship that warned you up front that they might not keep you on after three months." He paused, realizing this may be too much truth, "Look, I'm not trying to get your hackles up..."

"My hackles are fine, jerk."

"I'm just saying I think you should figure out who you are. Write about that."

"Nope, no hackles here, A-hole." She wouldn't even offer him side-eyes.

"Maybe a fictionalized version of you, Jane Walden, would bring about realization, epiphany, cognizance."

"You always try to diffuse me with fancy words." Jane pulled back her rising hackles, but wouldn't admit that to Christian. "But... you may have a point there, my fine feathered Christian. I've always read that a writer writes to find out what they think."

"All those online writing seminars paid off." Christian nodded his approval of her line of thinking as he took another shot of Fireball with an ice cream chaser.

"Maybe I can figure myself out by writing about me?" Jane finished.

"Bingo," he said, tapping his nose, indicating approval. "On the nosey."

Jane's face dropped. "But the problem is that I'm boring. Sure, I'm stunningly beautiful – she says ironically, but even I know I'm not that exciting. You gave me the Plain Jane moniker for a reason."

"It's not true. It's an ironic name, because you're *so* beautiful. That's why I gave it to you back in the day; my punishment for the un-charming Christian Jew thing you saddled me with."

She glanced sideways. "You do have a big nose..."

"Racist!" He screamed in mock indignation.

They laughed and clinked their plastic shot glasses, saluting each other with burning cinnamon.

He grabbed her laptop and opened it. "Aha! Let's see what the universe thinks of you."

"The password is..." she began.

He was already in, "Todd_is_hot. I know, you haven't changed it since forever. My God, you still use underscores. You really should change it. Wait... I'm not going to find naked pics of him, am I?"

"Those are on my phone."

"Gross."

"Maybe I should write about him." she glanced at the picture of Todd, the one formerly on her work desk. "My Gabriel Oak."

Christian stopped. "Oh no. Was that an obscure nineteenth century literary reference?"

She laughed, "Yes, I knew you would get that one."

"Ugh, Thomas Hardy. I hated that book. It should have been called *Far from the Maddening Whore*. She turned down fine Mr. Oak in the beginning, married the soldier jerk, then agreed to marry the old rich farmer, *then* welches on the deal and he ends up crazy. After all that, she married Oak anyway. I cringe at books where people can't make up their minds. Besides, Todd's more like the soldier guy that broke her heart."

"Are you kidding? I loved that book! Todd wasn't like Sergeant Troy," Jane started to remember Todd's numerous crimes, but pulled away from those thoughts. "And it's *Far from the Madding* Crowd, not maddening."

"Sorry, I feel I must correct all grammatical literary crimes. Thus *spoke* Zarathustra. Not Spake. Nietzsche was a dick, too."

"Well I guess you gotta make your stand somewhere."

Christian furrowed his brow at the laptop screen, and pushed his glasses back up. "Hmm. Well, you do pop up, but you aren't the only Jane Walden. Wow, there are a lot of you."

"Let me see," She laid on her bed next to him, staring at the screen, "Wait, look at all these pics. Oh my god, are all these women named Jane Walden?"

"I think some of the Janes are just standing next to Walden Pond." Christian arched an eyebrow. "Hold the proverbial phone. Jane, you've never Googled yourself?"

Jane thought about it, "You know, I don't think I have. Maybe I did when I was younger. But, I mean, look at all these women."

"A plethora of doppelgangers." He agreed.

"Oh my God, Christian." Jane jumped up and stood on the bed.

"What? Are you going to be sick?" He inched away, just in case.

"No…" She rubbed her stomach. "Well, maybe. But you're brilliant. This idea."

Christian rolled on his side to look up at her. "Idea? Which one?"

She slapped his butt as she returned to the bed next to him. "This brilliant idea! I took journalism. We ran the school newspaper together like dope editors, in high school and in college. So, okay. Maybe I *interview* other Jane Waldens. I learn their stories, I connect with them. It could be about the information age."

Christian helped, "A cool way to connect with strangers, across all socio-economic…"

"Yes! And about how women are the same, but different…"

"It could also be about self-discovery." Inspiration had smacked Christian, "*You* could be one of the Janes; tell your story. Wow. this could be about a lot of things."

"Yes! Ten Janes! Hmm, maybe five Janes. No, that's too few."

8

Christian announced, "Seven. Seven Janes. It's a stronger number."

"Yes! So, seven. That's good! Seven stories, all about other versions of me. Finding seven Janes...."

Christian countered, "Jane in seven parts. Nope. Sounds like a crime novel..."

Jane said, "The Plain Jane Same Name Game? No, that's dumb."

The light dawned. Christian smiled. "Here's your title: Seven Ways to Jane."

Jane stood and jumped up and down on the bed. "That's it! Seven Ways to Jane. I'll call up six of these Janes, do phone interviews. Or internet interviews, Skype maybe. Tell their diverse stories. A modern examination of womanhood, of connection, of how we see each other, see ourselves as modern women... well, something like that. I love it!"

"It's a good idea. You must do it, my dear." Christian did his rub-his-neck-deep-in-thought-thing again. "Wait – better idea - You should interview them in person."

"Yes! Christian... wait..." Janes face grew serious. She stopped jumping.

"What is it? No, don't stop. This is a good idea, you need to write this."

Jane covered her mouth and shook her head. She darted to the bathroom and made it just in time. Christian followed and made sure she didn't throw up in her hair, then made sure she got to bed. After the Snobar and Fireball whiskey finally hit them all at once, he then crashed on her cheap, squeaky, dangerously pointy Wal-Mart futon. Luckily, the idea survived the ordeal. For Jane, it burned hotter that the Fireball. This was exactly what Jane had been waiting for.

# Chapter 2

# Questing

"A bad beginning makes a bad ending." – Euripides

PLAIN JANE'S JOURNAL

*I'm broke. This great idea has a fatal flaw, and that's it. Zero money. As soon as my head began to function again this morning, I first said to myself, screw my boss and my dream job, then I paused briefly to look at the pictures of Todd on my phone. (Still can't delete those perfect abs.) I should have known from all the old Greek tragedies that the all those great-bodied gods are always assholes. Especially if they're named Todd.*

*Then this Plain Jane got to work.*

*Holy crap, there are a lot of Jane Waldens. Even several Jane Emma Waldens. But I'll stick to the just plain 'Jane Waldens' (pun intended – wait, is that a pun or irony? If I'm going to be a real writer I should know that. Anyway...). To find the most interesting stories, I will keep it a simple, high concept idea. Oh, I've also* decided to find a book deal as I'm writing. This is a great, marketable idea. How hard could it be? Okay, I'm kind of saying that ironically. But it is a great idea.

I've also stopped publishing the blog for now. I'm taking the blog on the 'down low.' Does anyone say that anymore? I am a jumble of pop-culture anachronisms. Anyway, I've gone old-school and began keeping a journal again - this is just me talking to me. I had a wild panic that someone would read my blog (one of my 227 rabid fans), and steal my idea. That may seem paranoid, but the message is active on my public blog that I'm going on a life changing journey and will publish what happened later. Hopefully with a book deal.

Then the fatal flaw returns. I'm broke. How am I going to pay for this journey? I barely have enough rent money for one more month at my crappy studio with the smelly carpet (no-matter-how-many-times-I-use-that-stuff-to-make-it-go-away!). I really need to look for another job. Now.

But this idea, though! It could be the idea that leads to fame and fortune – or at least my first book. I wrote a lot for my PR job, but I tucked away the writing dream all the way up into that corner next to my hopeless dream of a modeling career (Plain Jane for a reason, people). Now it's back. It's shouting in my mind, like an idea worm that will not die. This is all I want to do now.

Options? Sell stuff to fund the project. Problem – I don't own anything worth selling. I'm a California twenty-something that just got out of college last year. My parents have the money, and not all that much to *spare. Yes, I have thought about my parents. But they just paid for college. Besides, if my sister hears that I want to borrow money again, she will freak. Also, she'll smear on the guilt like a facial mask. Another flaky Jane idea. I don't need that right now. I still haven't even told my parents or sister about losing the "dream job," or that I have to move back home for a while.*

*Shit. Christian will know what to do.*

\* \* \*

Christian arrived at Jane's apartment. He brought coffee. "Why do we even call it coffee? There are seven ingredients in yours. Most of them made with sugar. Let's think of a new name: Sug-ofee."

"Hmm. Coff-sugee?" offered Jane.

Christian paused, "I like it. Coffsugee. That sounds familiar, like it should be a word. We're probably not the first to think of it. I better register the website domain name right now."

"Thanks for coming back after seeing me puke all over the place."

"No worries." Christian replied. "Not the first time. I went to college with you, remember? How's the idea coming?"

"Great," said Jane. "I found tons of Jane Waldens all over the United States. A few in Canada and at least one in England."

Christian sipped his own coffsugee "I think the kids are calling it the UK now."

"Whatever. Jolly old the UK. No ring to it. Anyhoo, the problem is money."

"Ahhh," Christian pushed up his glasses, "can't go on a quest without funds."

"Ooh. Quest, I like that. Any ideas? You're the smart one."

Christian smiled. "Thanks for finally acknowledging my genius. May I drink my coffsugee while I think?"

"Be my guest, sir." Jane sipped.

"While I'm thinking my brilliant thoughts, tell me about some of these Janes."

"Oh!" said Jane, putting her laptop onto her old bubbled-up linoleum counter, "I've bookmarked about a thousand pages. It's amazing what you can and can't find out about people these days."

"What do you mean?" Christian scooched next to her, to see the screen.

"Well, I found about thirty Jane Walden possibilities. Some of them have some pretty detailed information online, others almost nothing. Some, I could only find a picture or two. Can you believe some Facebook accounts don't have profile pics?"

"Aha. You've been stalking Janes all day."

"I have, and it should feel creepier than it does. Also – note with proper reverence that there are many towns, villages, cities and municipalities named Walden. There is even a Walden, Colorado. None of the Jane Waldens live in any of them. Here - I think she should be Jane number one." She clicked on a picture of a middle-aged Jane with dark hair and subtle highlights.

"Why her? What's her story?" Christian asked, sipping his coffsugee.

"I don't know the whole story." Jane wondered if she should tell him that this Jane just *looked* interesting. *Too shallow?* "She works in Vegas. But, I think the point should be that I find out her story in person. Find out these women's stories face-to-face."

"These *Janes*," corrected Christian.

"Right, these Janes. She has a Linked-In account that states she recently got promoted. The opposite of my career path, but a version of me that's focused on her job, at least."

Christian announced, "This calls for an epic cross-country road trip."

Jane countered, "But, again, no money."

"I see the problem." Christian sipped and thought, "A quest needs a sponsor – a patron of sorts." He smirked, one brow raised, "Hmm. I think I might have a way to pull off this little expedition."

"Really?"

"Maybe. Let's go see my Dad."

Jane lit up, "I love your Dad! You think he would? Wait, no, I can't ask your dad for money."

Christian winked, "I have something else in mind."

* * *

They took Christian's decade old car, the magnetic advertising sign with the "Golden Coast Brews" logo on both doors. He explained his strategy on the way.

Jane tried to get her mind around Christian's idea. "A road trip to sell your dad's beer?"

"Basically. You know how much he looooves you, 'Janey'. Your involvement could sweeten the deal. Sweeten and beer. Hmm. I apologize for the sloppy metaphor."

"I love him back. But why would he help me with this? I don't even know how much I need. Crap, I was so busy looking up Janes, I didn't even think of a budget for this."

"I did. I've been pitching a version of this beer-selling tour for a while. Not on this scale, but I have a spreadsheet or two prepared." Christian deftly reached behind Jane's seat and pulled out a file folder. A budget was inside. "I broke it down to gas, food, hotel stays, etc."

"Holy Shit." Jane scanned the document, neatly printed on an Excel spreadsheet. "This much? Abort! Abort plan! I'm going to apply for jobs right now," Jane said, whipping out her phone and clicked away.

Christian put his hand on Jane's wrist, curtailing the clicking for job sites. "Calm down. Listen, you know how much I love you, right?"

"Oh, I love you too. But this budget is ridiculous. Are you sure these numbers are right? No, of course they are. You were always good at math *and* English."

"I also make a mean Margarita – triple threat. The numbers are right. I ran them five times. I love you enough to level with you. That job wasn't you, Jane. You switched your majored to PR out of fear. Sure, you minored in English, but it was your real love. Hey, I'm all for a back-up plan. But you freaked out and I couldn't convince you to go after your first dream: to be a writer. I'm telling you now. Wrong career, wrong direction. Be a writer, Jane. Be like the old Nike ads - 'Just do it.' "

She put down her phone, "That was my number one PR firm. I was a good plan, not just panic. Besides, I still got to write… sort of. Their CEO gave my commencement key-note speech. I thought it was fate."

"The fate thing again. I think you might be looking in the wrong place for your version of fate." Christian replied, "I get why you did it. But it was wrong. You've been lost for a while. Heck, maybe we both are."

"Lost? Hey, buddy, I've been busy. They wore me out. I was 'adulting,' as much as that turned out to suck. At least the job had me writing every day."

"Copy writing, press releases. You haven't finished a short story since you started that job. I know you. You need the creative stuff. That job closed you off to what you really need."

She eyed him with crossed arms. From a Freshman psych class, Jane remembered that was a body language cue that the person wasn't listening, closed off. She uncrossed her arms. "Where's all this coming from?"

He looked at her, "How long have our fates been intertwined?"

Jane laughed, "You couldn't just ask, 'how long have we known each other?' Maybe *you* should write this book. You just slammed my belief in fate. You can't throw that back into the mix so quickly. I call metaphor foul."

"Well, I'm not the writer. I'm a better reader. I like the idea that our lives are intertwined. I'm a romantic, you know."

"I know. Remember when you sent, what was her name, that little hand broom?"

Christian smiled. "Ahh, Veronica. 'To sweep you off your feet.' I thought it was a good line."

"Then she posted that evil picture on Myspace, dissing you."

Christian shrugged. "Apparently, I'm attracted to shallow, bitchy, hot girls."

"In that case, you'd never be attracted to me."

"Not funny. My point, if I may veer back into the universe where my point may still be found, is that you pursued the narrow focus job plan that never once made you happy."

Jane crossed her arms anyway. "I was only there three months. I didn't have time to be happy."

"And you complained every day. I know, it was me who you called." Christian smiled.

"I called you mostly when Todd broke up with me for the umpteenth time."

"Ugh, Todd the Wet Sprocket. Screw him."

Jane chuckled, "Nice. Obscure Indy-rock Todd put down. You are on fire, my friend."

Christian looked over to Jane. "My point is, you need this. Pick up the old dream. It's what you are meant to do. We'll figure out the rest."

Jane answered, "You don't think we're a success yet? We're funny, awesome millennials that have college degrees and laughed off their bullies, right?"

"Yep, we showed them." Christian said, "You're unemployed and I work for my dad. Success!"

They laughed together as they drove into the complex of small warehouses, parking by the front office. They pushed through the glass door. The middle-aged woman behind the desk said, "Hey Christian."

"Hey Mary. Is Dad here?"

"Of course. He's in the back office, on the phone with The Wine Guy."

"Again?" Christian frowned.

Mary nodded. "Hi, Janey. How's your mom?"

"She's good. Still working at the bank. How are you?"

"Great. Say 'hi' for me," answered Mary.

"I will." They went into the warehouse, toward the back office. It was after five, so it was deserted except for the foreman, who smiled and waved.

"The Wine Guy." said Christian. "Great. I was hoping he'd be in a better mood."

"Who's The Wine Guy? You guys make beer, why is he an issue? Am I missing something?"

"Beer and Wine distribution come as a package deal. Haven't we talked about this?" Christian tried to keep the irritation out of his voice. "He's a total jerk who's breaking the rules and claiming he's not. He took over the biggest beer and wine distribution company in our area last year. Now he's not-so-subtly hinting he's going to drop us."

Jane gave him a quizzical look. "You have, like, an exclusive contract or something?"

"We did and do. When he bought the company, The Wine Guy bought the contracts. Each beer or wine producer can only have one distributor locally. Dad can't just sign up with several different guys at once. State law."

"And this guy's cheating?"

"More like being a thug. He's hinting that if we paid more, *maybe* he'd keep our beers on his list. There are so many wineries and micro-brews now, that we're having a hard time competing as it is. Now the biggest distributor might drop us. I keep telling dad to call the Alcohol Beverage Control – the ABC, but..."

They heard a raised voice, "... then I'm calling the ABC!"

Rounding the corner, Christian's dad was shaking his head, shutting his old flip phone. His face brightened as he noticed Jane, "Janey! Come over here!"

She smiled and let him administer his famous bear hug. He was a little pudgy, salt-and-pepper hair, with huge arms that wrapped around her. "Hi, Mr. Jacobson. How are ya?"

"Good. I'd be a lot better if you'd finally marry my son over there."

"Not cool Dad." Christian pushed up his glasses.

"I kid, I kid, I joke, I joke. Sit down," He offered them the two chairs in front of his ancient metal desk, right out a 1960's public school. Dad looked at Christian, "That was The Wine Guy again."

"We heard the tail end. Finally going to turn him in to the ABC?" asked Christian.

"Gonna have to. You were right. He'll drop us for sure now."

"Is that his name?" Jane asked, "Just 'The Wine Guy'?"

Dad elaborated. "No. It's Steve. He looks just like a Steve, too. Came out of nowhere, suddenly old man Martin sold the whole business to this Steve. I think 'great, all these shiny new trucks, young guy going to get my beers into more shops and bars, right?' Nope. The Wine Guy is a bully. Now, I wince when I see the trucks with purple letters and expensive graphics."

Jane connected the dots. "Oh, yeah, I've seen those around."

"Next time you see one, if you slash a tire or two, I won't turn you in." Dad changed the subject, "What are you kids doing? Christian, did you get all the website changes done?"

"Yeah, I finished them this morning. I scheduled the new site to launch at two am, so there'll be no interruptions or problems."

"Smart kid. You sure you don't want to marry him? He's single..."

Christian fired another warning glance, "Dad..."

Jane looked to Christian. "Wait, single? What happened with Sharita? You guys had been dating for what, a few months now?"

"Five. We broke up. I was going to tell you, but you had bigger problems. We'll talk about it later." Christian did some subject changing of his own, "Dad, I have an idea."

"Does it involve killing The Wine Guy? I think I could get a dispensation from the Pope."

"We're not Catholic. And no. It's about Jane here, and the business."

Dad arched an eyebrow. Jane realized for the first time the signature move was a family trait. "Okay, I'm listening."

Christian said, "We had been talking about new markets, expansion. Well, Jane has a project she'd like to do. I thought we could kill two birds with one stone."

"Rather kill two Wine Guys. Stones are optional." Dad offered. "Listen son, I'd love to hire Janey, but the budget..."

"No, no. Not that. I know Dad, money is tight. I was thinking I could start selling some of the new micro brews and Jane could tag along and work on her project at the same time. We would have to expense some stuff, but I could work on commission for any new sales I make, and the new sales would offset the cost of the trip."

"Sounds scary. What's this project, Janey?"

"A book - or a series of articles stitched into a book. I haven't heard back from any of my query letters yet."

"Query letters?" asked Christian, "Already?"

"I'm full of organized surprises. I'll tell you later. Now be quiet, I like your father more than I like you."

His father flashed his wedding ring, "Sorry, one time was enough for me." Christian shifted uncomfortably in his chair.

Jane jumped into flirt mode. "You're too young for me anyway. I like 'em in their early seventies, at least." Christian's father laughed. Jane elaborated on her idea, "Anyway, the idea is to interview other Jane Waldens across the country. Write their stories, show connectivity in the modern word, the internet, etcetera. It will be about identity, and telling gripping stories about powerful women who happen to have the same name."

Dad's brow went from furrowed to concerned. "Umm, the book sounds great. But you said 'across the country.'" He stared at Christian, "Kid, we've talked about this. We haven't even gone fully statewide yet. And California is huge. How far out do you expect me to jump?"

Christian blurted, "All the way to the East Coast."

Dad gave a nervous laugh, but Christian pushed through. "I know, I know that seems crazy. But Dad, if we don't go big and bold, jerks like The Wine Guy are going to keep kicking us around. Let's get around him, and take our brand national. We'd start slow at first, but imagine seeing bottles of Coastal Dude Brew being served in hip bars near Harvard, or a downtown nightclub in Manhattan."

"Manhattan, huh?" Dad shook his head, and spoke to Jane, "I knew this day would come. My little Christian showing his leadership skills, telling his out-of-date Dad what direction to take the company. Honestly, what he proposes scares the hell out of me. But really, I am so damned proud of him right now. You think I should tell him that, or keep it to myself?"

Jane, all smiles, replied, "Nah. Don't tell him. Stay aloof. You don't want this kid getting a swollen ego."

Christian pushed up his glasses, unable to contain his own smile. Dad swung his gaze back to his son. "You know we can't afford anything like that; you've seen the books. Hell, you put all the spreadsheets together." Dad sighed, "I assume you've got a round figure in mind?"

Christian handed his Dad the file folder with the budget, and several projection reports with graphs.

Jane said, "Holy crap, did you even sleep last night? In plastic presentation folders, no less? How did you even do this?"

Christian smiled wider. "I've been working on these ideas for a while."

"I'll say," Dad chimed in, thumbing through the reports.

"Plus," added Christian, "I was a business major before I switched to English, remember?"

"Oh, yeah, I forgot that," Jane answered.

"A cross country trip, huh? I rely on you a lot, son. How long would this trip take?"

"Two weeks, tops," said Christian.

"And that's quite the sum total," his Dad whistled at the cost. "I'm just a micro-brew, just a little guy, after all. You think the country will embrace our brand?"

"I do, Dad. We need to grow. Since Mom left all those years ago, we've settled for the status quo. It's time to grow. More sales could pay for new trucks, more staff. We could develop new seasonal flavors. Maybe become the next Sam Adams.

"Whoa, there. I'm starting to sweat." Dad fanned himself with one of Christian's reports.

"It's only two weeks, Dad. And you always say I need to get out there and have more sales experience."

Dad thumbed his wedding ring finger. Jane noted the sad smile. "I could spare you for a few weeks, I guess. It's the money, son." He shot his son a sad glance laced with a silent 'no.' "Jane, can I borrow my son in private for a minute?"

"Of course." Jane stood up and Dad came around for another bear hug. He thumbed his ring finger again, but consciously. "If you like him, you could put a ring on it."

"Dad! stop…wait, was that a Beyoncé joke?"

"I have a computer too, smart guy. I know what you kids are into these days with your Beyoncés and swing dancing and flapper outfits."

They all laughed. Jane left the room, headed to the front office to talk to Mary. Christian and his dad stayed in the back office.

Before too long, Christian walked out to the front office. He wasn't smiling.

Jane looked at Christian. Mary looked back and forth, totally in the dark.

She was secretly relieved. This book project idea excited her and overwhelmed her in equal parts. Jane put a hand on Christian's arm. "It's okay, I'll just call each Jane. We don't need to..."

"All systems go!" Christian's artificial frown changed to a smile.

"You jerk! He really said yes?"

Christian nodded. "I've got the time off, and the finances are all in order, kid. Let's do this."

Mary gave them quizzical, polite smiles as they said their goodbyes.

Jane chose not to be overwhelmed by the knowledge that she would now *have* to do this. The best strategy was to turn the tables and distract. Jane began hounding Christian on the way back to the car, "So were you going to tell me the whole plan? Or were you using me as a prop to soften up your dad?"

"Both." Christian smiled wickedly. "He loves you. But, if he said no, I would have had to go to Plan B."

"What was Plan B?"

"There was no Plan B."

"I see. So, you are a seller of beer now?" Jane mused, "I thought you just did the computer and IT stuff for your Dad."

"He's been asking me to do sales since I graduated. He's been teaching me some stuff. I've gone out in the field with our two sales guys, and Dad, of course, who is the best. Hard to say no to the guy that actually makes the beer, right? We need to expand. Dad's been stuck in a rut. A long rut. Plus, we have to find a way around..."

Right on cue, a large white truck with purple lettering and crisp photos cruised by, the overflowing wine glasses graphic splashed across the truck. "…guys like that!" Christian yelled, trying to match the loud rumble of the passing Wine Guy truck.

In the car, Jane asked, "So, are you sure your Dad can afford this? I don't want to cause trouble, or be responsible for hurting your dad's business."

"Too late. Your middle name is trouble," said Christian.

"No, it's Emma." Jane's eyes narrowed, "Yours should be Dick. Because you are."

"Yes. I both have one, and sometimes act like one."

"More importantly, what happened with Sharita?" Jane buckled up. "When were you going to tell me?"

"I figured it would come out on the road." Christian adjusted his glasses. "Things just didn't work out."

"She didn't cheat on you, did she? I'll punch her so hard…"

"You punch like a four-year-old child. She does Tae Kwon Do; Sharita would kill you." Christian stared straight ahead. "No, she didn't cheat. She wasn't *the one*, that's all."

"You're 23. Are you seriously looking for '*the one*' already? Then again, I thought Todd was the one, but well…" She didn't finish her thought.

"Enough of that. For both of us. No exes haunting our road trip. We have big plans to make. I want to be on the road in 48 hours."

"48 hours? Shit." Jane felt a rush of dizziness, peppered with panic. "Are we really doing this?"

Christian stared into her eyes. "Yep. Let's go sell some beer and write the great American book of Janes."

# Chapter 3

# Doubts & Ghosts

"A cock has great influence on his own dunghill." – Cyrus

"If once they hear that voice… they will soon resume new courage." – John Milton

PLAIN JANE'S JOURNAL
*We are really doing it! Christian has been amazing. He worked out all the money stuff, down to the last ducat and drachma, not that I understand spreadsheets all that well.*

*Confession: I got about halfway through breakfast when I had my first panic attack. What if this doesn't work? What if I come back with nothing? Just random scribblings about boring Janes that no one ever heard of. Who am I to write a book?*

*I've heard nothing back from my query letters. I thought this was such a good idea that I would get editors racing to my virtual door to sign me up for a fat publishing deal. I graduated from a good college. Okay – not Ivy League, but UC Santa Barbara is a kick-ass school. It got me my first paid internship. In PR. Which I lost. Shit, again.*

*Okay, stay positive. Think of that cute overly positive fish: "Just keep swimming." Or in this case, just keep journaling, in secret, no less. But, if only 227 people want to read my writing (my faithful blog readers), how the hell am I going to sell a book idea? I'm going over to Mom's later to inform her I'm moving back home, that I have no job, and that I'm going on a two-week road trip with my (and Christian's) brilliant idea.*

*Is this just a bad, crazy disaster in the making? Can I do this? This is crazy... Okay, I'm cussing and using exclamation points and ellipses. I hope that's not a bad sign! I need... I need some affirmations, and quick, before I face Mom.*

\* \* \*

"I just want to understand this *completely,* Janey." said Barbara Walden, Jane's mom.

Jane grabbed another trash bag full of clothes from her back seat. "It's just a glorified road trip, Mom. Me and Christian. Wait, is it Christian and I? I should know that if I'm going to be a writer... anyway, it's two weeks doing these interviews, then I'll write the book. I might write the book while Christian's driving, like, as I go. I haven't decided."

Mom carried a bag to the center of the garage. "Then, you'll look for a job when you get back?"

"Yes, Mom. Well, probably. It all depends if I get a book deal or not."

"Is it really that easy?" asked Mom.

"No, of course not. I'm just trying to stay positive. I've been doing some research on query letters, submitting book proposals, but there is so much info out there. I've sent some queries out already, so hopefully this amazing idea will get a positive response. I just need a little encouragement right now."

Jane's sister Cathy pulled up in a green Prius.

"There goes my encouragement," Jane whispered under her breath.

Her mom didn't hear it, or pretended she didn't, as Mom was already walking to the Prius. The door opened and Cathy Walden-Ganton got out. She hugged their mother professionally, not disturbing her own makeup or hair. She swept around the car when she spotted Jane.

"Janey! Why are you here?" She cocked her head behind her oversized sunglasses, noticing the pile of stuff now occupying the otherwise neat garage. "Oh no, is Janey in trouble again?"

"Hi Cathy." Jane resisted the urge to spit the name out. She reminded herself that she wasn't twelve years old anymore, that her older sister had no power over her. "Yeah, little Jane screwed up again and got fired. Oopsy."

Mom got the last small box from Jane's trunk. "Now girls. Be nice. Cathy is just concerned. Did you really not tell your sister about losing the job?"

"Mom, I just told you. I haven't had a chance. The idea and this trip, it's happening really fast." Jane immediately regretted saying too much. "I was planning on calling you, Cathy. Wait. Why aren't *you* at work? Can they live without you for even five minutes?"

"It's my lunch hour, silly. I just wanted to make sure Mom was bringing the cake for Saturday. Oh, I was going to text you. Are you bringing a plus one for my birthday? Christian, I assume? You know it's at one o'clock this Saturday afternoon, right?"

"Oh shit. I forgot. Listen, about that. I can't make it. I'm going out of town."

"You're going to skip your sister's birthday party?" Mom asked, "Why can't you leave after?"

Cathy removed her sunglasses. "What's going on?"

Jane was cornered.

"Oh, Janey is going to interview other Jane Waldens all over the country and write a book about it... instead of looking for a job."

"Wow, Mom. Passive aggressive, much? It's a little more complicated than that. It's also about Christian, who is helping his dad's business by selling beer all over the country. He'll do his work, while driving me around for my project."

"Writing a book? That's an ambitious project. Have you put a book proposal together already?

Written a killer query letter? Have you got a current list of Literary agents and what they're looking for?"

"Yes!" Jane snapped, but pulled back. "I mean, of course I've been doing that. What do you know about any of that, anyway?"

"You know my friend Deborah. She's been trying to get published for years. Finally went the self-publishing route. She was always telling me stories of how brutal it is out there. She even showed me a few of her rejection emails. And she has an MFA in writing. Of course, her book is on business, a non-fiction thing. But, good for you for trying something new."

Jane stiffened so she wouldn't literally deflate like a balloon with her sister's "helpful" information. She quickly replayed the last sentence a few times, deciding whether to respond to the words, or the underlying condescension. Jane decided to keep it all surface with her sister.

Jane smiled widely. "Awww. Thanks, sis. I appreciate the encouragement." Jane went to give Cathy a big hug. Her mom stopped her.

"Janey, don't be sarcastic. Cathy only wants what's best for you, just like your Dad and me. Oh, I better call him about you moving back in. Excuse me girls." Mom walked off, through the garage and into the house to call their father.

"Are you really going to miss my birthday?" asked Cathy.

"I am actually sorry about that, but Christian has a timetable and has already mapped out the trip. I honestly just forgot. But, you won't miss me anyway.

I usually just sit in a corner with Christian and judge all your friends."

"Judge Jane and her not-boyfriend, yeah I've noticed. Well, I'll miss you. And John will miss Christian. He really likes him. But he'll have a few other husbands to hang with. How does Todd feel about this trip?"

"It's been over with Todd for a while."

"Oh, I didn't know." Cathy said. "You never tell me anything."

"Well, you're busy."

Cathy smiled. "I really am! I can't imagine adding kids to the mix."

Jane paused as the new information hit her. "Wait, are you pregnant?"

"No. Not yet. But John and I are trying."

"Of course you are." Jane folded her arms. "Why not add one more thing to your perfect life? Wait. No. That sounded petty. Of course, I'm happy for you."

"Oh, Janey. Yours will happen. Must admit though, I will miss Todd's hotness. That boy had a great ass. But hey, maybe you and Christian will finally get together."

"Cathy! Stop it. He's just my friend. Always has been."

"I don't know. Behind those geeky glasses, he's pretty cute."

"Quit it. Anyway, I gotta go." She gave her sister a real hug. "Trip stuff to do. Sorry about your birthday. I'll pick you out a gift on the trip."

"Okay, little sis. Be good."

Jane hopped into her now empty car, watching Cathy walk into the house. Jane drove off, thinking of her older sister's fully formed life. She hoped to get out of town without any more emotional delays. She thought, *now for the fun stuff – buying junk food for the road.*

* * *

Jane turned around on her way to the checkout line; Todd stood in her path.

In front of the convenience store coolers, she'd gripped the six pack of energy drinks, now cradled in the nook of her elbow. She didn't notice the cold against her skin. Jane was suddenly too warm.

She thought, *did he notice me flush? Do I care? Wait, am I flushed...?*

He broke her metal distraction by saying, "Hey Jane. I thought that was your car."

Words didn't come. *He got his hair cut. Probably this morning, probably from that bitch hairstylist he's with now. One of the many girls he cheated on me with.* She realized she hadn't replied in way too long. Jane also noticed her eyes running over his arms, chest, finally resting on his abs. Her eyes moved a bit lower, when she brought the iron curtain down on those thoughts. She managed a stilted, "Hey, Todd."

He didn't respond right away. Todd looked at her with his sparkling green eyes, wearing that movie star smile that would look like a smirk on anyone else. He just stared. "Special celebration, or regular party?"

She was confused by the question when she finally registered the energy drinks. She shifted the cold drinks to her other hand. "That stopped being any of your business, *Todd.*" She emphasized the last work like she always had when she was mad at him. It never worked; subtle criticism seemed to bounce off chiseled Greek gods.

"Yeah, I guess you're right." he replied.

Jane wished Christian was here. He would never fight Todd, of course. He just seemed to be able to affect whatever spell Todd always cast on her. *If I hadn't volunteered to get the snacks...* she thought, keeping her eyes firmly on his, "Where's – what's her name – Maleficent, or whatever, the one that cuts hair."

Todd laughed openly, like they were friends again. "She's, umm, well..."

"Uh oh, trouble in paradise?" Jane quipped, "or paradise lost?"

He wasn't laughing anymore, but held that not-smug god-he's-gorgeous smile.

Jane wanted to swing all six cans right into his beautiful face. She resisted the urge. "I would say that's too bad. I'm not going to. I have to go, *Todd.*" He smiled. Nope, still didn't work.

"I know. I just saw your car and I needed to say something."

"I don't want to hear it," she lied, not moving.

He took a step, his abs dangerously close. "I just... I'm just better with you."

A tingle shot through her neck first. It began to travel other places before she made them stop. She managed, "That's not fair."

"I know. None of this is fair. I ... listen, do you think...?"

*We could strip right here? Go back to your place and 'talk' about it? Have sex with no strings?* She was sickened by the idea that none of these ideas made her angry. It was his low, totally man/boy voice mixed with his high school jock good looks that seeped into her resolve. She hadn't been this close to him for so long. His smell...

"No, Todd, no." Jane took a step back. "You broke up with me. You cheated on me. You blew it. I gave you enough chances." Jane surprised herself with the words, and the force behind them.

Jane thought he would try to touch her. She still didn't try to walk away. He put his hands in the pockets of his jeans. The action made her glance down again. *Thank God. I don't think I could have resisted if he touched me.*

Todd's smile appeared again, but mixed with something else. He nodded his head with acceptance. "I understand. I just wanted you to know that. You were the best. I don't deserve another chance."

"Oh... okay," her feet came loose of the tractor beam, though she noticed her legs felt wobbly. "I have to go."

She didn't look at him again, that now remorseful, resigned face. She paid with plastic and rushed out

the door, forgetting anything else she was supposed
to get.

Jane drove away, but of course she glanced back.
The moment was over. *Damn him. He does not get
to do this to me.* Then she remembered Bathsheba's
refusal when Gabriel Oak proposed to her. She had
refused her Oak and had to go through lots of mistakes until she got her man. Before fate took her on
her circuitous journey back to Oak.

Jane thought, *screw this narrative.* Jane drove to
Christian.

# Chapter 4

# Jane #1

"In this life, one must have a name; it prevents
confusion even when it does not establish identity."
– Ambrose Bierce

PLAIN JANE'S JOURNAL
*Last rent paid (barely), crappy apartment cleaned, de-
posit promised to be returned by mail, minus carpet
cleaning. Bags packed. I'll drive over to Christian's, so
my car will be safe while we're gone. Saved all the six
Janes' info to hard drive in case internet is spotty. (I also
wrote them down - very 20<sup>th</sup> century of me, I know.)*

*Note: sent out twenty query/proposal e-mails to lit
agents and so far, two outright rejections, and deafening silence from the rest. Okay, now all I have to do is
jump out in to the world with no job, no real money of
my own, no promise of this book leading to anything,
oh, and no guarantee that –*

1) I can really write this book (my Mom and Christian love my writing, but they don't really count, right?), or

2) That any of these Janes will be any more interesting than I am. But there's one cool thing: Jane #1 is in Vegas, baby.

Okay fate, you better help me out. Your track record hasn't been real great lately, but all is forgiven if we can become buddies again for this trip. I am taking deep breaths. I am resolute. I am strong. I can do this. Oh shit, here we go...

* * *

Jane arrived at Christian's room shortly after the Todd incident. Christian had had his own place, but moved back in with his Dad a few months earlier. He said it was to help Dad with the business, but Jane knew it was also because of his college loan payments and other bills. Christian seemed more on edge than usual.

"Hey. You're late," he chided, but with a subtle smile.

Jane replied, "Tardiness is a constant enemy I'm still trying to vanquish." Jane pulled the last bag out of her car. "But I'm here, and I think I have everything."

"Cell phone charger?"

"Shit."

"Jane..."

"Just kidding. It's right here. I'm ready. But, I do need a big strong man to help me with my bags, though. I'm just a helpless young girl..."

"Sounds like the opening scene of a porno film."

"Ha! We're taking your dad's car?"

"Yeah, he insisted." sighed Christian. Jane noticed he's put his dad's car key on the San Francisco key fob she'd bought for him years ago.

Jane laughed as they went for her bags. The trunk opened and Christian blanched, "Holy shit. This trip is supposed to take two weeks, not a world tour in the 1880s. Might as well have brought a steamer trunk and a caravan with an elephant rifle."

"It's not that bad," Jane said, "I'm just glad we aren't flying. These bags are way over the limit."

"We are literally on a beer budget. I have to keep the fridge cooler in the back seat to keep it plugged in, and my bag is small. Four bags, Jane, really?"

"Not four. Count them: Two suitcases. One's a purse, the other is my laptop."

"Is that a magical Hermione Granger bag?" Christian quipped. "Or a carpet bag from the civil war?"

"Wow, okay Mr. Christian, that's a lot of referencing all at once."

"That's right: history buff and English major. You know, because both are so useful in today's world." He considered, "Well, I guess we can put one of the bags in the backseat with the cooler."

"I know you'll make it work." She smiled the winning smile that always softened him up. "you're my rock."

"Yes, I'm aware," groaned Christian as he lugged the bags into the car.

"You seem testy, beyond the bags I mean. What's up?"

He loaded the last bag, "I'm just feeling guilty. My Dad can't say no to me, I know, and definitely not to you. This trip will help sales, but he really can't afford to have me away for so long. If I don't deliver..."

"But you will. Remember how you talk me out of things I can't afford all the time? We'll just do that in reverse. I'll be your support team. We can do this."

"I'm just a little worried, that's all."

Jane smacked his arm. "That's what you do, old chap. It's one of the many reasons I love you."

"Love you too, but with these bags we'll be getting about ten miles to the gallon. This trip had better work, for both of us." Christian settled the rest of the stuff, pushing up his glasses as he got into the driver's seat. Dad had insisted on them taking his trusty Sebring. It was roomy, and as old as his failed marriage. But Dad rightfully pointed out that 1) Christian's second-hand Festiva might not make it across country, and 2) To quote his dad, "My car's old, but I do every schedule maintenance item on the list. It will run forever." As they got into his dad's car and settled in, he hoped his dad was right. A wave of doubt brushed through Christian as he pondered the stakes of this trip.

Jane put out her hand. "We're really doing this, Mr. Christian. Let Fate be on our side."

Their hands joined. "Yes, we are doing this, Miss Plain Jane Walden. I hope this fate you keep going on about is real."

The pact finalized, the quest began.

Christian mounted the portable GPS on the glass, and programmed the Vegas destination. The kind female voice calculated the trip from the Central California Coast, through the tip of messy Los Angeles, until they would finally be on a nearly straight shot to Highway 15 into Vegas. Fate showed up, but they would never know it. She would be hiding in the GPS device. Fate would be watching Jane very carefully along the way. It would be a very interesting trip for both of them, in ways they never would see coming.

On the road, Jane caught Christian up to speed, "Okay, Jane number one: she's thirty-seven and works for a large time share company."

"What does she do there, exactly?"

"I don't really know. I thought I'd find all that stuff out in the interview. I want to be surprised by what these women are all about. I 'talked' to her through Facebook messaging."

"Is she excited to talk to you?" Christian glanced at the GPS. All was well, and they were firmly on track.

"She's a bit leery, I think. The first thing she brought up was identity theft. Hadn't thought of that. I guess working in Vegas forces you to see the shady angles. She now understands the idea, what I'm trying to do. I said I would contact her again when we got close to Vegas. What will you be up to while I see Jane number one?"

"I set up three meetings with local beer distributors. Two are not far from the strip, so we won't be traipsing all over Nevada."

"Good word use. There's not enough traipsing these days. Do I get to taste the beers?" Jane asked with a big smile.

"Nope, you old alchy. Besides, you've been drinking my dad's beer since we were both way too young. These samples are strictly for the prospective clients. I've got a range of our four brands: Coastal Dude Brew, Delta Red, Pale Phantom, and Dark Tumbler."

"I love me some Dark Tumbler. Hey, I just noticed most of those names are kind of, I don't know, intense? Funny, since your dad is so laid back. Have you ever told me the story there?"

"Not sure, you seem to forget a lot of what I tell you." Christian said, shooting a look to Jane.

"Do not... sorry, what was your name again?" Jane countered.

"Funny. Coastal Dude Brew was the first beer, invented in the happy days of the marriage. Delta Red is a nod to the fact that my dad was in the military. The others were named after mom left. Since she still gets a slice of the business, I suppose we should be grateful they aren't called 'Alimony Ale' or 'Bitch Brown Bitter.' "

"You are quick today," Jane laughed. "Ever think about talking to your mom? It's been years, right?"

"Let's not begin on a bad note, please." Christian lost all his mirth. "No talk of that woman. You know the rules."

"You know I've always thought if you patched things up with your mom, you might have better luck with the ladies." Jane shrugged. "Just saying."

"Thank you for your opinion. I will file that in the appropriate place." Christian pretended to take a piece of paper and flush it down an imaginary toilet, complete with sound effects.

"Jerk!"

"I am sometimes." Christian changed the subject back, "And yes, I like Dark Tumbler best too."

Jane nodded, letting the mom issues go for now. "You do like your beer like you like your women."

Christian arched a confused eyebrow, "Thick?"

"Dark…"

"Racist!" he screamed in his familiar mock refrain. "wait, was that a dig at Sharita's skin tone?"

Jane ignored that. "…and dangerous, of course. What degree belt did she have in Tai Kwon Do?"

"Green belt. Hmm. You may have a point there. Not like I have a ton of experience. I've only slept with three women."

"You've slept with me." said Jane.

"Didn't count. Yes, we slept – well, passed out drunk after a party is more accurate. But I mean sex. We haven't done that."

"We certainly haven't." Jane considered the number, "Three women. Really? Huh."

"What, you don't approve?" Christian looked over his glasses at her.

Jane tilted her head. "I'm just surprised. I mean, I don't want to imagine you having sex, of course."

"Thanks."

"You know what I mean, but I assumed you'd had more than three women." Jane reasoned. "I mean, we are best friends and still there are things you never talk about with me."

"True. I've always thought male and female 'besties' - wait, no – let me retract that stupid word – that *best friends* should keep some subjects off limit. But this trip feels like the time to fix that." Christian pushed up his glasses. "Damn. I knew I should have got these glasses adjusted before the trip. Anyway, nope. Just three. Do I want to ask the same question of you?"

"Umm. I guess..."

Christian looked over, "Well?"

"Still counting," Jane said as she pondered. Christian looked back at the road, then back to Jane.

"Shit, Jane. Are you still counting?"

"Sorry. Just making sure. Seven. What a coincidence. Seven Ways to Jane takes on a different meaning."

"It's a fateful trip. Seven, really? Okay."

"Hey! Don't judge. I like sex."

"Everyone likes sex. But seven? When did you find the time? Did I meet all of them?"

46

Jane countered, "You gotta prioritize. Wait. You said three for you. I know Caitlin was your first. You were seventeen, right?"

"That's the story. Good selective memory. Sweet Cait. But she moved away and it sparked out. Couldn't survive the distance."

"And Sharita, I assume, recently. Who was number three?"

'Actually, I never told you about number one. Cait wasn't the first." Christian looked at the road.

"She wasn't? How dare you keep these things from me." Jane feigned offence.

"Well. It's just… I was sixteen my first time."

"Scandalous!"

"Kind of. You remember my mother had that friend Lilith? She came around for years after Mom left. I'm sure she wanted my dad. But he wasn't interested."

"Holy shit! It really is scandalous. You screwed a cougar?" Jane laughed.

"Lilith was only thirty-three, and she was super-hot."

"How did it happen? I thought that only happened in sex comedies or porno flicks."

"It was like a porno." Christian laid out the story like a screenplay. "Dusk. Exterior shot of family home. I hear the doorbell. Dad's at work. She stands at the door with a lasagna. No doubt trying to hook my dad through the food angle. I had just gotten out of the shower, towel wrapped around me."

47

"Oh my god! Delivery for... oh my, what big muscles you have young man, etcetera?" Jane laughed through her surprise.

"Dad and I had the lasagna that night, and I had a big smile on my face for days."

Jane belly laughed, "I'll bet. Why didn't you tell me before?"

"Gotta have some secrets, nosy. A gentleman does not discuss these things." He almost stopped there. "Finest blow job I ever had."

"Christian!"

"I wasn't very *Christian* that day."

Laughter peeled from Jane. "Why did it stop?" Her laughter slowed down. "Wait, I just realized, all boyhood porno fantasies aside, that was a sexual assault."

"One of the reasons I don't talk about it." Christian said, "Nowadays especially, it's even more awkward. It was only that one time. She hinted a few more times, but it ended up kind of reminding me of my mother after that. I was angry for a long time, as you know."

"Actually, I don't really know. You never talk about her, one of your rules. I barely even remember her. Why did you never patch it up with your Mom? I mean it's been, what, like ten years?"

"Again, let's make the car a mom-discussion-free zone."

Jane persisted, "Has she tried to contact you?"

He relented, a bit. "She used to. Nice try, but discussion closed."

"Okay, okay. Sorry. Anyway, we can stop now. Besides, I really don't want to imagine you having sex with a criminal cougar."

"Again, thanks. I think."

Jane finished, "But, you need some more experience, kid."

Christian shrugged, "Well, it's very nice of you to throw yourself at me, but I must decline your wanton advances at the present time."

The laughter set the tone for the first patch of their duel quests. Settling in, they drove in silence for a while. Jane was getting drowsy looking at the desert stream by on either side. Before she rested her head on the passenger side window, she squeezed Christian's arm. He smiled and patted her hand. The thoughts of mothers and old flames, and cougars drifted away with the scenery.

Jane awoke when she felt the car slowing. She stretched her arm and smiled at Christian.

Christian pointed at the sea of cars and red tail lights ahead. "Vegas, baby. There's the traffic to prove it."

Route 15, the highway to sin, always congested the closer it got to the city, despite the five lanes. They saw shiny gold buildings and the iconic glass pyramid. The traffic slowed from 70 mph to just under 40, despite all the lanes.

"Shoot. I better message Jane Number One," she said, looking for her phone in the door cubby hole. She fumbled, grabbed the most important thing in her life and tapped away at the screen, "Okay, I hope

49

she's a fast responder. I hate when... Oh I got two e-mails to the writer account."

"You set up a new e-mail? Smart," said Christian.

"Yeah, just for this project, lit agents, etcetera."

"Why don't you send your idea directly to publishers?"

"Oh, I wish it worked that way." She read the e-mails on her screen. "Maybe it did a long time ago, but now publishers only take submissions through literary agents. I must get one of those first... and from this very nice form rejection e-mail I received, it may be harder than I thought. Oh, the second one is more personal. It says, 'Thank you Miss Walden, we like your idea, but feel we could not sell your writing until you have more experience.' Then this little gem of encouragement, '...but the publishing world is very subjective, with only 1% ever getting through the process. Good luck.' "

Christian offered, "Well, at least they gave a reason."

"Holy crap," Jane looked up, like a lightbulb exploded overhead.

"What?"

"Christian! Could they just take my idea and have someone else write it? Do they do that? I never even thought of that."

Christian considered her worry. "You mean, you fear you'll see next summer's 'must read' called *Seven Ways to* Janet, written by someone else?"

"Oh my God! What's to stop them? I went blog-quiet to avoid this very thing. I need to get this done.

If I finish the book fast enough, no one will have time to steal my idea, right?"

"It shouldn't be that dire. There must ethical standards in the literary business." offered Christian.

"You mean like that Wine Guy?" Jane countered.

"Shit, you may have a point." Christian said, "How many e-mails did you send out?"

"About fifty!"

The GPS voice interrupted them to tell them which exit to take. Fate wanted to tell Jane that most literary agents operate with a high moral and ethical standard. She also wanted to explain how hard it is to break into publishing in this new modern world where everyone can publish their kindle masterpiece and sell it online instantly. Instead she announced, "In half a mile, take Tropicana exit, on your right."

"We're almost there," Christian reassured. "One problem at a time, kid."

Janes phone dinged, "Oh, and look at that, Jane One responded just in time. Maybe it's meant to be. Thanks fate."

The GPS did not respond.

Jane calmed down. "Okay, panic attack over… for now."

"You sure it's okay if I drop you off, and come back for you? It's my first out of state sales call."

"Of course, I'm a big girl and the first Jane Walden is expecting me. Hmm. That sounded like I was talking about myself in the third person. Jane is not amused, Jane says 'off with her head'."

"Crazy girl."

"And you love it."

"Yes, I do," confirmed Christian.

They were lucky that they got to avoid the Vegas strip. The GPS lady delivered Jane to the High Desert PMI Resort. It was nearly three blocks away from, but ran parallel to, the Vegas strip. Christian dropped her off, and left for his first sales pitch.

Jane came through the thick sliding glass door of the resort and the temperature dropped by forty degrees. Leaving the hot dry desert air behind, she approached the woman at the desk. The petite lady in her early twenties asked how she could help.

"I have an appointment with Jane Walden."

The receptionist smiled. "Of course. What name may I give?"

"Jane Walden, actually." Jane thought, *this could get awkward quick.* She blurted, "I'm writing a book about other Jane Waldens, like, connecting with people in our digital age."

"I see," said the woman as she picked up the phone. She spoke for a moment, hung up, and showed Jane down the large corridor. "Right this way, please." Jane noticed the expensive high heels the woman wore. *This place is built to impress, even down to the details,* thought Jane as she was led back to a fairly small office. As the receptionist knocked on the frosted glass in the door, Jane pulled out her phone, "Oh, is it okay if I take a picture?"

"Of course," said the woman professionally. Jane clicked a picture of the name plaque by the door that read Jane Walden, Account Executive. The reception-ist swung the door open, then quietly left.

"Hello." said the Vegas Jane, getting up from her desk. "Come on in." Vegas Jane was trim, with healthy curves just under her dark blue jacket and pants. She swept around her desk professionally, her pony tail perfect, no hair out of place.

They shook hands, Jane noting how firmly Vegas Jane shook hands. *A common trait in the business halls of Vegas, or just her personality?*

"Thanks for giving me some of your time," Plain Jane began, "I'm sure it seems kind of strange."

"It's fascinating, actually. You know, I never really thought about other Jane Waldens out there. I got your message and Googled myself. I was shocked at how many of us there are in the world. Did you know they even have a word for it - Ego surfing?"

Plain Jane nodded. "I did come across that phrase in my research, though I haven't really had a lot of time – this has all happened pretty fast. Of course, I never would have thought of this idea if my friend Christian and I hadn't been drinking, and wallowing in my recent firing... wow, I am just babbling, and just way over-shared. Sorry, this is new for me, too."

Vegas Jane smiled and lifted her hands to the window behind her. "Sin City." Plain Jane saw a glimpse of the Vegas Strip between the open blinds. "Nothing shocks us here. Sometimes a few drinks with your friends can get the creative juices going. Of course, most dumb-asses visiting the strip take it way too far."

"Yeah, I bet." Jane took in the view. "I've been to Vegas once before, but too young to enjoy it all."

"How long are you staying this time?"

"Only today, actually. Kind of a whirlwind trip. So, thank you so much for meeting with me. I'm sure you're busy."

Vegas Jane flashed a professional smile, like the receptionist. "No problem. Not too many fires to put out today. How does this work? Has the interview started?"

"Umm. Yes, it starts now," she got out her spiral notebook with lined paper, "I want to ask you some questions, but also feel free to just talk about your life, your interests."

Vegas Jane glanced at her notebook, "Lower tech than I expected. I thought you'd ask to record me or something."

"Oh! That's a great idea. My phone doesn't have much space for audio. I loaded a lot of music on it for the trip. But thank you... maybe I should've invested in a recorder."

Vegas Jane eyed her, patiently. "Sounds like you're still working out the plan."

"Yeah, sorry. This is happening fast – idea, straight to action, like, super speed. I'm hoping that will keep the self-doubt to a minimum. But I do have some questions written down, at least. First, what is your job title and where were you born, your general background, etcetera?"

"Well, I only have about 45 minutes, so I'll try to be succinct. My official job title is Executive Account Manager. I'm the person who coordinates all of the 'meets' with prospective buyers, then coordinates the clients when they purchase."

"This is a time-share company, right? People rent out, like, one week a year at your hotel?"

"Actually, you just used a few words we hate in the industry. We don't rent anything. You buy Real Estate here. Our system uses points. Those points entitle you to so much time in a resort – not hotel – resort, that you own like real property. You pay property taxes, and you can pass on your property to your children."

"Wow, That's really interesting." Jane quickened to add, "I hope my assumptions didn't offend you."

"It's okay. Lots of people think as you do. It's my job to line up the sales team and teach people what time share ownership really is. The great thing about our resort is that it's in Vegas, a very sought-after spot. Instead of staying here with the points, which would entitle you to stay for one week, you could stay in other popular properties in Hawaii for the same amount of time, or stay for two weeks in our beautiful, but less travelled, Ozarks resort.

"I see. Interesting. And what... how? Sorry, why *this* industry?"

"You mean - what was my career path?" Vegas Jane smiled.

"Exactly. You are my first Jane. I will get better at this. I feel like I'm stepping over my own awkward phrases."

Vegas Jane stood. "I'm honored to be your first Jane. Let's make this a walking interview, shall we? That should shake off your nerves. Then I can show you what I do and you can see how this other Jane lives and works."

"Awesome. That would be great."

Vegas Jane took her to the top of the resort, beginning with the Presidential Suite on the 32$^{nd}$ floor. "Wow," was all Jane could say as they strolled through the four-room suite. Dazzling crown molding towering above high-end paintings and furniture. Vegas Jane answered the peppering of questions, filling in her life path to Vegas.

".... After getting my BS at Ohio State, I ended up in radio advertising for a time, which took me to Florida, which led to eventually walking into one of the largest time-share companies in the world – a lot of time shares in Florida – but then I moved up the chain with PMI International, and was shipped out here."

"You live in Vegas full time? Quite a change from Florida, I'd imagine." Jane continued scribbling her notes.

"In some ways, yes. Still a big city, just like Orlando. Both places are hot. Please note, it's not a joke about 'dry' heat. It's very different than Florida's sticky wet mess. I won't miss the giant wild bugs either. Plus, *this* is the view from the top," said Vegas Jane, opening the drapes to the balcony. "Not scared of heights, I hope."

"Holy Shit!" Plain Jane caught herself, "Oh, sorry!"

Vegas Jane laughed, "It's okay, that's what I thought when I first came up here."

Blocks from the strip, at floor 32, the Vegas strip was laid out for them. Close by she saw a black pyramid, a hotel shaped like a castle, the torch of Lady Liberty, and what must have been the faux Eiffel tower. Her only family trip to Vegas, when she was a teenager, was mostly spent in the pool at their hotel. This was something else. Vegas, baby.

They headed down to the bottom floor through a series of large rooms. By that time, Plain Jane found out that Vegas Jane had two kids: Maggie and Johnathan, and a husband that worked at the highest level of security management at Bally's Casino.

The family lived in Summerlin, a suburb of Vegas, twenty minutes outside the city, and their lives were generally happy, but as Jane secretly feared, not particularly interesting. Vegas Jane shared her ambitious nature. *Maybe that's the angle*, though Jane.

"This is a very competitive business, and my next step is to become VP of the western region. It's two pay grades up, both now occupied by men. But I have a five-year plan."

"I thought I had planned. Then the dream job went poof. And the boyfriend. My Oak."

Vegas Jane tried to understand. "His name is Oak?"

"No, sorry. It's from the novel *Far from the Madding Crowd*. He's the guy the heroine eventually ends up with."

"I see," Vegas Jane crinkled her brow. Jane didn't know what this meant. It was a small, vague "tell," in poker terms. She didn't pursue the Gabriel Oak thread, but kept the tour going "This is the sales floor, where we welcome the new property owners, and they get their free $100 in gambling money for listening to our pitch. But I won't bore you with that stuff. What else do you want to know?"

"Sorry, I kind of swung the conversation to me, didn't I? Thanks for your patience with me today. I see that you are the tough, competitive business Jane. I guess what I want to know most is - how do you balance it all? Do you feel like you're a step closer to your dreams?"

"Oh, Jane," said her Vegas version, laughing openly. "this is not the dream. This is just work, a way to make money. The dream is being with my family, living a life. Taking my own vacations. Hopefully, not screw up my kids too much with all my long work hours. Yes, there's a balance. But I try to keep my eye on the real ball: my family, my life."

"Really? I thought... well, I had you pegged for the tough in the boardroom Business Jane."

"Oh, I am. But I'm a lot more. Is that how you're going to write it? Each Jane with a label? I'd be careful with the easy assumptions until you have the whole picture. I don't want to be portrayed like a caricature"

Jane was taken off balance by the comment, "Oh. Well, yes...I guess that is kind of a trap I could fall into."

"Before I forget, are you planning to use my real Company's name? I'd have to check with legal if you are. Do you have any sort of waiver you'd like me to sign?"

Our Jane felt a trickle of perspiration. "Gosh, I hadn't... hadn't thought of that. Do you think I need a waiver?"

"This is Corporate Vegas, Jane. There are lawyers and paperwork everywhere. I would check into it. But don't worry about me. You can use everything we've talked about. Obviously, you can use my real name - that's the point. But if you want to use the real company name, I'd have to get the okay, that's all. You have my contact info. Your publisher will probably take care of all the legal stuff, anyway. But, you should probably think of some of these details. Keep *your* eye on the ball, Jane." she winked.

It didn't comfort Plain Jane, whose mind was already making new mental to-do lists for herself. "Okay. I think I'll just generalize about timeshares as far as the name goes. I will get back to you with follow up questions, though." Plain Jane buried her face in notes, scribbling furiously.

"Jane, can I give you some advice?"

The question felt like Vegas Jane had lifted fifty pounds from her shoulders. "Please."

"You may want to think through some of these details before you see the next one of... well, us. A Jane Walden myself, I can tell you that being organized it your best friend. This is a big thing you're doing. I hope you've considered all the work it's going to take to do it. I know nothing about the publishing world, but my mantra is about keep your eye on the prize – but make sure you've examined it from every angle. You are the boss of this project. Don't let it overwhelm you." Vegas Jane finished with that professional smile.

Plain Jane felt a little smaller than when she entered. There was a lot to think about. She chewed the inside of her lip, a new habit that was beginning to annoy even herself. "You're right. You've been great, and given me a lot to think about. Thank you so much. It was great meeting the first other Jane Walden. Is it... is it okay to take a picture with you?"

"Oh. Yes, of course. Jane Walden to Jane Walden, shoulder to shoulder."

Jane used her phone for the picture, and took several shots.

Vegas Jane shook her hand, "I wish you all the luck. Let me know if the book is ever published."

"Oh, it will be." Plain Jane declared, "I'm a little scattered, but I'm determined." Jane said goodbye to Jane and made her way to the concrete parking structure attached to the building. She pulled out her phone to text Christian, but he was standing there with his hands in his pockets. "Hey Plain Jane. How'd it go?"

"Onward Christian soldier," Jane continued scribbling new ideas. "I'll tell you in the car on the way to the strip. I need a drink."

"Jane, you know we're on a budget."

Side eyes were flung at Christian. "One drink in a Vegas Casino won't break us."

Christian rolled his own eyes, but hopped in the car willingly enough. Fate thought Christian should be more assertive. He was the driver, after all. The GPS told them how far it was to Bellagio Resort in a measured voice. Fate was excited. She had always wanted to see the famous fountains up close.

"The Bellagio is the one with the fountains, right?" Jane asked.

Fate sighed inwardly.

"Yep, just like in that heist movie Ocean's Eleven. Always wanted to see this hotel. Let's go pretend we're rich for a few hours."

Although the strip was only a mile away, it took them over an hour, due to traffic. Jane recapped the first Jane. ".... In the end, she was encouraging, but there were some issues that came up, which shook me."

"The legal stuff?" asked Christian for clarity.

"Yeah, and it wasn't just that. It was her tone. She was so on point, that it kind of, like, freaked me out. It was like my first Jane is my mentor, but I felt totally unprepared in the moment. At the end she said 'if' the book ever gets published. I just feel, like, off balance now."

"That's seventy-five cents to me," announced Christian.

Jane asked, "What?"

"I'm going to start charging you a quarter every time you use the word 'like.'"

"This again?" Jane went into her valley girl voice, "Like, it's really like hard to like not use the word like, I'm like a millennial, after all."

Christian tallied up the verbal crimes. "Buck twenty-five more, please. At least you're not letting every last word of a sentence go up in inflection."

"Like when everything sounds like a question? Like all our friends talk? How can you not find this, like, charming?"

"Just give me a five-dollar bill as collateral. You're hopeless." Christian asked, "Do you want to hear about my day?"

"Of course, yes! I'm such a jerk." Jane focused on her best friend. "How'd you do?"

"Fifty-fifty success. Got a 25-case commitment from one distributor. The other one liked the samples, but turned me down. He doesn't like California's bureaucracy. He's right. California is nuts, especially their booze laws."

"Wait, I don't get it. How is your dad going to deliver to Vegas, anyway?"

"Oh Janey-Jane, you weren't listening to the plan. We'll set up a quarterly delivery. One long haul with one truck to deliver everywhere I sell on this trip. That was the hardest thing to sell to my dad, actually. He's scared of change. This could be a big deal for us, if I don't screw this up and give him a heart attack."

"That sounds like a lot of work." Jane said, "But I know you can do it. I believe in you."

The GPS made a strange sound, something akin to a scoff. Christian turned it off.

Christian announced, "I called Dad already."

"Was he excited?"

"Proud of me through a miasma of unspoken worry." Christian shrugged, "I wouldn't say excited."

"Okay, dude. 50 cents. I'm going charge you each time you use a stunning literary phrase. Or a pretension one. They come in equal measure from you." She smacked his arm. "My confidence had already taken a hit today. Maybe you should write the book."

"Now, now. You're the writer, I'm the Jane cheering squad. I didn't mean to sound pretentious. It's just, with my dad – I don't know... he loves what he does, always has. But that woman leaving stuck him in this weird time-warp. He knows we need to grow, expand the business. It's his confidence that woman took. I want him to take it back."

"Maybe you need to work out some issues with you mother." Jane suggested, "Maybe that will inform how you can help your dad."

Christian gave a non-committal shake of the head. Apparently, the subject was closed. Instead, he smiled and held up his hand. "But you know what? Golden Coast Brew just made its first sale outside the state. Screw you, Wine Guy!"

Jane slapped his hand for a well-deserved high five. "Success! You're a marvel Mr. Christian. I love how much you love your Dad."

"He's a good man. He just picked the wrong woman." Jane heard the grit in Christian's teeth. She wanted to get at that knot. *Surely, his mother issues are holding him back.*

Jane offered, "Hey, they got *you* out of it. That's pretty awesome."

"Thanks. I am pretty awesome. Glad you noticed." Christian smiled wryly. "Anyway, it's not a silver bullet, but it's some cash flow for dad."

"Well, we have no worries tonight, Señor Christian."

"Still randomly trying out new accents, El Patrona?"

"Si, mi hermano. Let's get a drink and get ready for Jane number two."

# Chapter 5

# State of Nice

"In the smallest comic details lies the universe." – Holly Hunter

*Okay journal,*

*What the heck is in Nebraska? Wait - Does that sound uber-Californian-snobby-elitist- of me? Probably. Need to watch that, Plain Jane. Remember, this is going to be a national (maybe international) best seller. Can't make people in the bread basket angry. Bread Basket? Do they still call it that? I shall do some Google research.*

*Then again, no one may want to read my super exciting, character-driven almost-novel about interconnectivity and mirror-image self-obsessing. Maybe I should broaden it – include the millennial road trip angle? If I keep getting deafening silence back from all the literary agents, I'll have to spice it up somehow. I sent out another ten queries. Nada, nothing, zilch. Stay positive, #realjanewalden. Note: I just made that hashtag up.*

*Anyhoo, Jane #2 is in Nebraska. The state website says "Visit Nebraska. Visit nice." I think I like that. But is nice just another word for boring? Jane Walden Two lives in Scottsbluff; small population, but close to larger city. My Facebook stalking revealed a husband (local politician on the city council), and her job is in local retail. Plus, a super adorable- four-year-old named Wyatt.*

*I'll call from the road to confirm, but it looks like we are off to see some "nice."*

\* \* \*

"Off to Nebraska - the state of NE," said Jane loudly.

"Why did you pronounce it like a word and not an abbreviation?" Christian held out hope. "Are you making a cool Monty Python tie-in joke?"

"Who is he again?"

"Get out of the car!" Christian mock-yelled. "My Dad and I love Monty Python – 'we are the knights that say nee. And we demand a shrubbery!' "

Jane thought she remembered. "Is that one of the weird old British comedies you made me watch?"

"I tried. Apparently, you weren't ready. Python is a master's class of funny. And it's a comedy troupe, not a guy – like Pink Floyd is a band, not one person."

"Okay, classic comedy and rock references? And I thought I was the scattered one. Pick a hobby, buddy. From now on you are simply Christian: the English major helping his dad with his business. Stay in your damn lane, dude."

"Crap, I do sound pretentious sometimes, don't I?" Christian countered, "As long as I can start a swear jar, potty mouth. We'd be millionaires."

Jane sighed, "Yeah, well, that jar would be filled with IOUs, buddy."

Christian noticed the gas gauge. "That reminds me, gotta fill up again, get fresh ice for my samples."

"Are they going to last all of these states?"

"If you don't drink any, ya lush. Don't worry, I'm a good planner," said Christian. "Unless I do more tastings than I thought, which is a fine problem to have."

Jane smiled, reached over and squeezed Christian's knee.

"Shit!" Christian swerved, Jane laughed.

"I knew you were still ticklish there. Now you have to contribute to the swear jar."

"Imaginary swear jar. You think you know me so well, huh? What's my favorite color?"

Jane answered back, perhaps too fast, "I know that! Let's see…"

Christian started humming the Jeopardy theme song, "Time's almost up."

"Green. Shit, no, that's dumbass's favorite color."

"Which one?" Christian pushed up his glasses.

"What do you mean *which one*?"

"You've dated a lot of dumbasses." Christian knew it came off as judgmental. He didn't care.

Fate smiled to herself.

"Hey now, don't judge. I meant the last dumbass: Todd."

"Ahhh. That dumbass."

"Hey, wait, are you calling me a slut, Mr. I've-only-slept-with-a-few-women? Are you a millennial prude?"

"No, of course not. It's not about frequency. I'm just saying you have terrible taste in men. You gravitate toward jerks."

"That's not true!" But she was quiet for a minute. "Geez, you're right. Todd, Spencer, Alberto..."

"Don't forget Scott and Bobby."

"You remember Bobby? That was like eleventh grade."

"Still counts."

"Am I really one of those girls?" Jane chose the phrase carefully. "Bad boy magnet? I always yell at those girls in books and movies."

Christian nodded. "That's why I'm here, to keep you honest."

"What about you? Let's see, they didn't make the sex list, but there were a few other girls I remember - there was Jennifer in high school. I remember her because she was so sweet."

"No, she wasn't. She was sweet to your face. She hated you."

"Really? Wow. She fooled me. I've usually got a better radar than that." Jane was genuinely surprised at the betrayed memory. "Why did she hate me?"

"Jealousy. That was her main emotion." Christian smiled. "However, her biggest problem in my teenaged opinion, was chastity."

"Aha! Didn't make the sex list. You guys really never...?"

"Nope." Christian shook his head. "We did some stuff, but never all the way."

"That sucks for you. Wait, how did we get into a conversation about you and sex again?"

"Just luck, I guess." Christian pointed. "We are now in Nebraska, by the way."

Jane looked at the sign, *Welcome to Nebraska*, but decided it was too late to snap a picture on her phone.

Christian asked, "What exactly are you going to ask this Jane? Have you refined your questions? Or are you trying different questions with different Janes?"

"Good questions, all. I thought a lot about that actually." Jane dug out her notebook. "Should I keep a standard list of questions for each Jane to show the vast differences in their unique personalities, or should I tailor the questions to their unique walk of life?"

"And your decision?"

"My decision is that I have no idea."

"Super. Sounds like a plan." Christian smiled but he was also shaking his head. "Nope. That is the exact opposite of a plan..."

They arrived at the modest sized town and used the GPS to find the two-story home. The home was obviously built in the last 15 years and resembled many of the newer construction housing tracts that you could find in any part of America: sandy earth tones with little character, but wholesome and well kept. Jane made a mental note to try to make this part of the narrative; that so much of America looks like so much of the rest of the country. Christian decided to go with Jane to the door. His few sales stops wouldn't take long. Might as well make introductions now, instead of randomly popping in later.

A woman in her late twenties came to the door. Her smile was her leading feature. This Jane Walden smiled widely in a way that some people do when they're pretending to smile. Plain Jane could tell immediately that there is nothing phony or pretending about this woman.

Jane Two said, "Hi. It's so nice to meet you. Come on in."

Our Jane replied, "Thank you for agreeing to see me. I know this must seem strange, just messaging you out of the blue."

"This is such a cool idea. I couldn't say no."

"Oh, this is Christian," Our Jane motioned. "My road buddy and best friend."

"Nice to meet you," said Jane Two.

They were led into the spacious three-bedroom home. Jane noticed that even the personal belongings seemed familiar. Perhaps like they'd been bought at a big box store that supplied the same items to all their stores across the country. A large man in a suit entered.

Christian offered his hand, "Hi. Christian."

"Peter. Nice to meet you. I'm not sure my Jane has ever been interviewed before. She's really excited."

"That's true," Jane Two confirmed. "Peter's used to being interviewed, because he's on the council, but I'd get too flustered at a reporter's questions. This is different."

"I'll make it easy," said Our Jane, "No pressure. I'm new at this too."

"Shall we go into the dining room?" suggested Jane Two.

Christian demurred. "Actually, I have to be off for a few errands."

Peter seemed interested, so Christian elaborated, "I'm trying to help with the family business by spreading California microbrew beer all over the country."

"Awesome. I love beer. What type – Pilsner, IPA, Lager?" asked Peter.

"A man who knows his beer," Christian approved. "Lager and IPA. What's your favorite?"

Peter laughed. "Anything cold. Most politicians around here drink like Prohibition's coming back."

If there was danger of ice, Peter had broken it. "I'll see you out," said Peter, "Honey, I have to go to the office for a while anyway. That'll give time for you two Janes to chat."

Just then, a boy darted into the room. He'd obviously been coming out to tell his parents something very, very important, but the strangers made him skid to a halt. His pajama bottom feet slid on the carpet and he almost ran into the wall.

Peter caught him. "Whoa there, big W. Slow down. This guy is Wyatt. Big W, this couple of visitors here are Christian and Jane. Say hello." Peter put Wyatt down.

The four-year-old stood up to about Christian's waist. He looked at the two strangers with wariness, and shyness won the moment. No hellos. He darted back down the hallway.

"That crazy kid" said Peter, "Big W's a little small for his age, but he makes it up in energy."

"Yes, he does," added Jane Two as she glanced down the hall after the boy.

Peter kissed his wife and waved to Our Jane. Christian and Peter left out the front door.

"Why don't we sit down? What kinds of things do you want to ask about me?" Jane Two motioned to the chair.

"Well," Jane noticed a painted wooden sign on the dining room wall. It read: "sometimes the most precious thing is in front of us." She thought of Wyatt. *That's it. This is Mom Jane.* She dug out her notebook again, thinking wistfully that she should have taken Vegas Jane's advice about recording the conversation. Too late now. Notes would have to do.

They sat at the large dining room table. Jane realized she hadn't spoken for a moment, too much in her own head. "Sorry. I like that saying on your wall. The book is called *Seven Ways To Jane.* In other words, meeting other Janes with my... *our* shared name. I still have to get used to that. It's mostly learning stuff about your life. Then we'll see how seven different

72

Janes live in modern America. I'm still working out the questions, so maybe you can help me figure it out a little, too. You are only my second Jane, so we can just have a conversation."

"Okay," Mom Jane nodded. "Got it. Shoot"

"Great. Why were you named Jane? Does it run your family?"

"No," Mom Jane said, "my mother liked the movie *Somewhere in Time* with Jane Seymour."

"Oh, that's interesting. I wonder how many of us nowadays are named after actors and actresses?" Jane made a note. "Okay. What do you do for a living, and do you like it?"

"Well I'm a full-time mother and a part-time worker over at the Ace Hardware. It's a small family chain that has a few franchises. They take good care of their employees and they work around my schedule with Wyatt," as if summoned, the boy appeared like a shot. "Pardon me a second. Wyatt? What are you doing, buddy?"

The boy darted around the corner again with some oversized Lego knockoffs in his hand, "Building a castle," he said. His shoulders shrugged as though no further explanation was needed. He ran back down the hallway with building blocks in hand.

Our Jane exclaimed, "That kid is seriously adorable. If you were in California, every casting agent in Hollywood would want to hire him."

"Yeah, we kinda won the lottery on that one. I mean, Wyatt is a staple at every public event Peter attends; he's much more popular that me and Peter.

73

Plus, he's such an easy kid. He's a bit shy, and a picky eater, but he's the love of my life." she winked at Our Jane. "Don't tell Peter that."

"I won't," Jane smiled, an air of conspiracy. "Umm, okay. Family stuff: where are your parents from, ethnic background. Basically, where do you and your family come from?"

"Peter and I are both mutts through and through. I know I've got German, English, Dutch and a little bit of Native American. Not enough to get any oil or casino money, unfortunately, but we think Choctaw. Always wanted to do one of those new DNA tests you see on TV, but really can't justify the expense. Doesn't really matter much to me anyway. I mean, it's the 21$^{st}$ century, we'll all genetic mutts now, right? My family's mostly from around here. My mom passed on, Dad is still around and I have one sister who lives in Oklahoma."

"You're a natural at this interview stuff." Our Jane felt more in the interview groove. "Do you like being married to a politician?"

Mom Jane chuckled. "Well, that requires a politically correct answer."

"Hmm. Intriguing," Our Jane arched a brow.

"I don't really like the attention. I guess Wyatt gets the shyness from me. It's alright for the most part. I stand there and let Peter shine. We go to a lot of local events, get seen, all that. But this is a fairly small pond. No real drama."

"And you've never done interviews, for local papers and stuff?"

74

"Luckily no." Mom Jane realized the irony of her disliking the idea of interviews, "Oh, no offense. This is totally different. Peter does all of those. Being interviewed by a writer is actually kind of exciting. I don't know much about you real writers. Do you have an agent or a publisher in New York?"

"I wish! I mean, not yet. I'm actually working on getting an agent while I'm doing interviews." Jane admitted, feeling a bit like a fraud. She mentally waved away the doubt.

"Wow. Sounds tough. A lot of work and worry."

"It's a little scary, if I'm honest." Our Jane resisted the urge to chew on her lip. "I've already gotten a few rejections, just based on the idea. But I knew rejection would be a big part of this. Anyway, I'm focused on the positive. Sorry, enough about me. Next question - why Nebraska? Why do you live here as opposed to anywhere else in the world?"

"Well, family, of course. But, I just love it here. I know a lot of folks yearn for adventure and other places, but I always yearned for this." She motioned around to her neatly organized home. "Peter's a great guy, Wyatt's amazing and we don't miss any meals. We could move. But why? I'm pretty darned happy. I read my romance novels and we take trips at least once a year, often out-of-state, just to get away."

Our Jane made notes, but secretly hoped for a more interesting Jane. *No, that's mean. There is nothing wrong with a happy woman.* Mom Jane sensed some hesitation.

"I've been to France," Mom Jane announced.

"Now that's interesting." Our Jane perked up, a little ashamed at the same time. "When did you go to France?"

"Five years back. It was only for a week, but Mom always wanted to go. She couldn't know that the cancer would get her the next year, so it's a Godsend that she was able to make that trip. We went on the cheap, except for a couple of nice meals. She loved it. I did too, especially sharing it with her. That was special."

"What did your Mom do?"

"Housewife, worked part-time in retail, like me. But, my Mom was a 'yearner,' for sure. She always read books and novels set in foreign places. But reality... well, in the end, the sickness got her pretty quick. Liver. She was gone in four months. Cancer is a careless monster."

Our Jane was surprised by this poignant memory, and wasn't sure how to handle it. She instinctively turned to a positive question, "What did you like most about France?"

"The best part of the trip was seeing how much my mom loved it. She wasn't touristy about it, she didn't run around and chat everybody up and pester folks with questions. She just absorbed. Mom walked around like she was in awe of everything: the buildings, the museums, the cobbled streets where we found them, even the modern buildings. She cried at the Eiffel Tower."

Jane made her notes not looking at her hand. Some emotion from Mom Jane had caught her attention. *She's gone quiet, lost in memory. Do I disturb that, or let it happen?* Her subconscious answered, and Our Jane prompted, "Just the two of you? Your dad didn't go? No Peter?"

"No.," she said it as though Jane should have known the answer. "Peter had his work and he was nice enough to take care of things here at home. This was before Wyatt, so it was easy enough. I'm guessing he ate a lot of fast food while I was away. My Dad's afraid to fly. He's a great guy, my dad. He didn't mind us going off on our own. I know *Dad* ate a lot of greasy burgers that week."

"Sounds like it was a great experience," Jane didn't want to interrupt the narrative, but she felt Jane was faltering.

"It... it was. But, for me, it was a nice place to visit and all, but it was so old and closed off. Even though there are lots of young people, especially in Paris, it all just seems dull somehow, grey. I know that sounds strange. I mean, I live in Nebraska, right? You know, maybe we aren't the most picturesque state; we don't have Rocky Mountains or oceans or many things that some of the states like California have. But I've seen other places. And this is pretty nice, you know? It's home."

"Well, I can't get a better answer than that." Jane tried one of her new questions. "You may already have answered this, in a way, but what is your dream?"

"My dream? Hmm, my dream. A lot of my friends left here. You know, small town kids, but they had to get away right after high school. In fact, I'm sure I had the same feelings in the beginning; dreams of getting out. I had friends that wanted to be actresses or wanted that big job in politics or to be a lawyer at the high-profile law firm. Peter is certainly driven, but I don't think he'll go much farther in politics. Maybe the State house, although he may secretly dream to be President. I wouldn't be surprised if that was in the back of his mind. But he's too nice. I think to go past a certain place in politics you have to be some stripe of bastard. Peter's not that. As for me, I see the people that have these A-type personalities and I kinda feel sorry for them. They never seem to be really happy. Never fulfilled."

Our Jane smiled politely. Mom Jane realized how it might sound, "Oh no. I wasn't talking about you. Big dreams are great. A real writer? That's excitement. But... and I don't want to sound like I'm a throwback to some old-timey era. Honestly, I'm living my dream life. I feel pretty fulfilled. Is that wrong? Sometimes I feel like some women think it's wrong to want this. But I love my life." She leaned in conspiratorially, "Well, honestly, a little more sex wouldn't hurt."

Our Jane laughed involuntarily.

Wyatt came around the corner, this time with a stuffed animal that looked like a fluffy cat. Mom Jane was pretty sure he hadn't heard anything about the "more sex" line, but she burst out laughing anyway. This made Our Jane laugh harder, which made Wyatt laugh even though he had no idea why he was laughing. Wyatt's mom extended her arms and he came into them. She hugged him hard, then he started to wiggle. He thought he was going to his mom, but she had turned into a fearsome tickle monster. He squirmed and giggled and received a merciless tickling.

"You ready for the rodeo tonight, Big W?" Mom Jane continued tickling. She looked at Jane, with her own armful of Wyatt. "Oh, do you and your fella want to come?"

Our Jane was startled. "You mean Christian? Me and Christian? Oh no - he's not my fella. Very nice to invite us, though. I'll have to ask. But, I don't think we have any plans tonight."

"Good. Of course, you're sleeping here tonight." It wasn't a question. Wyatt giggled in Mom Jane's arms, fighting for escape, but also wanting more.

"Oh. Wow. Well, we haven't got a hotel yet, but... No, you don't even know us. We couldn't impose."

"Don't be silly. We have a spare room just for occasions like this. To make you feel better we'll charge a $10 Airbnb fee."

Our Jane raised an eyebrow. Mom Jane winked. "We have the internet out here in the bread basket."

*It is still called the bread basket.* Jane thought about Christian's worries over money. She said, "That would be great. I'm making an executive decision. We'll stay."

"Good. I'm glad."

Wyatt escaped the tickle monster that was posing as his mother. Christian returned a short time later and Jane told him of the new plan of staying with the family. He was noticeably relieved not to need a hotel. He'd made no sales that day; two of his appointments canceled outright. So, an inexpensive hanging-out with a nice family sounded good to them both.

* * *

Peter was back by four and they decided to eat at the rodeo fairgrounds. Peter insisted on driving. There was plenty of room in the SUV and Wyatt liked having Christian and this new Jane as guests in his backseat. Wyatt became quite the chatterbox. He told Christian all about his online mine craft adventures and Christian wasn't sure if he was telling him a story that he had made up or was from some cartoon that he had seen. Christian decided to play along was the best move, so he nodded and exclaimed at the proper times.

Jane had never seen Christian interact with a child before. It was an interesting intellectual exercise to imagine what he might be like as a father, so cerebral in his thinking and analytical in his approach to things. Jane decided offhandedly that Christian would marry some beautiful engineer or mathematician and together they would produce a baby genius. Jane would end up hating them all, of course, for their collective perfection.

She was glad for the unique experience of the rodeo, even though she had no idea what to expect. They arrived and got waved through a dusty road to a gravel parking area. An older man who wore a bushy mustache and red handkerchief confirmed they were on the right path with a wave. It was a sea of cow-boy hats.

Wyatt unbuckled, they all got out and follow the crowds to the fairgrounds. Peter took on the role as guide, between waving to people that he knew (which seem to be about half the crowd), he explained that the fair and rodeo had been going since 1956. The fairgrounds were a multiuse facility used for lots of events during the year – but this was the biggest annual to-do.

As they walk through the fairgrounds, Peter pointed to the different areas: livestock grounds, trophy area, the arcade Gallery with carnival style games and rides. There was food everywhere, both by local organizations and traditional, purpose-built carny trailers selling everything from hot dogs to fried Twinkies. Our Jane was more than a little surprised to see fried pizza, and a hamburger that had sugary doughnuts substituted for the bun.

Jane decided to follow the family and have ham-burgers and fries – not the doughnut bun style – just the regular kind. Christian had a chili dog. As they finished, it would be about 35 minutes until the rodeo itself started in the stadium stands and rodeo ring. They made their way over to get good seats. When they settled, Christian asked his new best friend Wy-att, "Is this your first year at the rodeo?"

Wyatt hopped to his feet, "Nope. Last year we saw the motorcycles."

"Motorcycles? At a rodeo?" Christian cocked his head. "Are you telling me a story again?"

Wyatt shook his head side to side so hard that it moved his whole body, "And there were 'splosions!"

Christian looked a bit concerned until Peter explained, "They do a lot of horse riding maneuvers, wrangling, roping, stuff like that. At the end of the show they bring in ramps and there's a motorcycle daredevil show. In fact, Wyatt, buddy – I hear they're signing autographs afterwards."

Wyatt gave a comical look of disbelief. Christian laughed freely. He wondered what the actual value of an autograph would be to a four-year-old. His face suggested it was worth billions.

Christian obviously enjoyed the experience of this "family of nice." Jane noticed Christian smiling openly. She commented to Peter, "Interesting. I didn't think motorcycles and horses would mix well together."

Peter adopted a wildly exaggerated Southern accent, "Well, shucks, you know us countryfolk; Nascar, cowboys and explosions. White trash entertainment, aint I right, ma?"

Jane detected a little more intensity towards the end of the statement than lightheartedness. She wondered again about her project and how it may seem like these "know it all Californians" were invading the lives of others, or worse, condescending and judging them.

Our Jane saved the moment from awkwardness. "Well you know us stuck up California types with our…." she adopted a specific upper-crust character, "…Chardonnays and indecently condescending superiority." She laughed at her own silly voice. So did Peter, luckily.

Christian assisted Jane. "We really appreciate you guys letting us hang out with your family." Peter give Christian a nod and a smile that seem to defuse any potential landmines. Jane reminded herself that Peter was a politician, and wondered how genuine his smile really was as he smiled back at her.

The sunny afternoon turned into the evening. The stadium lights came on, and the show ramped up. They had a great time watching all the tricks the riders performed. Jane was very concerned about the roping of the young steers. Peter pointed to the young ones, trussed up by two ropers. He noted they were let go right after, no lasting harm done. Jane relaxed. She was surprised at how "into" the action she got, gasping as the young riders got thrown, cheering as the ropers did amazing feats at full gallop.

Christian glanced over to Jane often, exchanging many glances. They were both having fun. The two Janes sat next to each other and had quite a good time chatting about things that Christian couldn't hear. Wyatt had adopted Christian and was talking his ear nearly off about everything that came out of his young brain.

As promised, ramps were pushed onto the field and they were treated to a motorcycle show with two daredevil stunt riders. They performed amazing tricks. The stadium didn't seem big enough for the wild flips off the curved ramps. Jane noticed with alarm how short a landing time they had before they had to decelerate. But every move was flawless as the ramps stood opposite each other. The two motorcycles even did loops in the air at the same time passing each other with what look like only inches of clearance.

Then the tour de force of the explosions started with pyrotechnics just like a hard rock metal show. Fireworks also shot off in a grand display all over the stadium, highlighting the ever-increasing higher jumps. One was dressed in a neon green jumpsuit and the other in bright red, though they were nearly blurs at high speed.

The crescendo of fireworks exploded as the riders came down for their final landing. The crowd went wild, exuberant. Jane and Christian couldn't help but participate in the standing ovation. Wyatt had been jumping up and down the entire show and even though it was over, he seemed as satisfied as any four-year-old ever could be.

It didn't feel overly crowded, until it was time to leave. Everyone left at the same time, in the same direction, so they all had to shuffle along slowly. They stopped and got out of the crowds when they realized that the motorcycle performers signing autographs was behind the stadium bleachers, in the opposite direction.

Fighting the crowds, against the flood, took a while. They finally found the line of two dozen people waiting for autographs. Wyatt peeked around the legs of everyone in front of them to see glimpses of the two riders sitting behind a plastic folding table.

When they finally reached the young daredevil riders, Wyatt was suddenly, painfully shy. They purchased an 8 x 10 of each rider, and a trading card size glossy shot of the two riders in midair. Both the young men couldn't have been more than 21 or 22 and were very nice to Wyatt. Wyatt the former chatterbox, lost his voice in front of his new heroes.

He stared as the two riders signed the card. They invited him for a photo, a selfie with the riders. Wyatt would have none of that, until the last second when he suddenly agreed. He stood there, between the young men, seemingly about to bolt. When the two riders put their thumbs up, Wyatt did the same just in time for both Janes to snap the shot on their phones.

Wyatt clutched the trading card. Peter showed him how to hold it, careful not to smudge the fresh autographs. The crowds had thinned, but they could see the long line of headlights pointed out the only exit road from the fairgrounds. They finally got to the SUV in the parking field. It took nearly an hour get out of the fairgrounds. Wyatt fell sleep in the car within five minutes of being buckled into his car seat. Jane slyly motioned for Christian to look over to Wyatt and saw the angelic four-year-old, still clutching the trading card in his hand like a treasure never to be relinquished.

Finally, on the road, Jane was thankful for the lights of the highway that flashed by sporadically, so she could make notes on the experience. They got to the family home and were shown to their room. Christian's stomach was a little upset at the overindulgence of his chili dog with extra onions. They had a private bathroom and realized that the guest bedroom only had one queen-size bed.

"I can sleep on the floor, or the couch in the living room." Christian said while brushing his teeth.

Jane dismissed the thought. "Don't be stupid. Boy and girls can sleep in the same bed without having sex."

"Hmm. I'm dubious." He peered over his glasses. "How do I know you won't attack me in the middle of the night?"

"Ha! You wouldn't know what to do with me, no offense."

"Oh, offence taken. But maybe you're right, seven other guys. Not sure I could keep up with that experience level."

"You have a charming way of *not* calling me a slut."

"I never would, because you're not. Plus, it's not polite." Christian rubbed his belly. "But I think I'll reluctantly take you up on the offer. I don't want to have a stomach ache *and* sofa-inspired back problems at the same time."

"You and your delicate stomach."

"Nonsense. I eat crap all the time." Christian still held his belly. "I just overdid it on the onions."

"Then I hoped you scrubbed those teeth good, dragon breath."

Christian said lightheartedly, "Oh, I sleep buck naked by the way. Is that a problem?"

Jane spit up some toothpaste at that, "Shut up, I saw your pajamas laying on the bed . Good choice, by the way; red lips over a black background. Very Rocky Horror Picture Show. Nice." Jane finished in the bathroom, sat on the bed and made some notes.

"We should leave early tomorrow. Next is Wisconsin. You meet with Jane number three the day after tomorrow, right?"

"Correct, sir," Jane said as she rubbed her eyes and closed her notebook. "You know, Nebraska was a lot more fun than I thought it would be. It should make a 'nice' chapter in the book. See what I did there?"

"So clever, you. Have you given any more thought to what this book is actually about?" He said, sitting next to her on the bed.

Jane was surprised by the question. "You know what the book is about – meeting other Janes as an example of modern America, femininity, and connected-ness."

"Is that all it's about? Isn't it also about self-discovery?"

"What do I have to discover about myself?" Jane furrowed her brow, and stared at Christian in his hot lips pajamas.

"Well...," Christian cleaned his glasses, avoiding Janes stare. "I was just watching the other Jane tonight. You two were chatting. And I got to thinking about you."

"I'm calling her 'Mom Jane,'" by the way. Warmer than a numbering system." She reluctantly got back to his point, "Alright. What about me?"

"Well, isn't this a bit about trying to find out who you are through the eyes of other women that might have been you, under different circumstances." Christian continued, "Yes, the gimmick is that the names are the same. That's the way into the story. Like you say, this is 'Mom Jane,' the first was 'Business Jane,' who is also a mother – paths you might have taken, or may still. But maybe there's more to be said about you?"

"How, exactly? It's a nonfiction project that will have some narrative elements. That's the idea I'm pitching with the book proposals. Sure, I'll throw myself in there as the seventh Jane. You think it's the wrong way to go?"

"No, no." He clarified, "not necessarily. I just don't want you to miss the most important Jane in the book: you."

"Hmm. I hadn't really thought of it that way."

"It's just a thought." Christian said as he turned off the lamp on his side of the bed.

"Well, poop. I can't decide if you just gave me a better idea, or a poison pill."

"Sorry. Just crossed my mind. Goodnight."

Jane reluctantly turned off her lamp. Jane worried that she would not be able to sleep. *Is this about more than I think?* That was a last thought she remembered before she drifted off. It felt good to have someone else in the bed again, even if it was only Christian.

# Chapter 6

# Deep Waters

"We can't manage what we don't understand and we can't protect what we don't know." – Diva Amon

PLAIN JANE – SUPER JOURNALER

*Damn you, Christian. Damn you to hell. I take that back. Of course, I love you, buddy. But you have put the inception of the idea in my head. Now I can't stop thinking about it. You gave me this stupid idea in the first place – "Seven ways to Jane." Now, you changed its very nature.*

*What is the book about? Well, going to be about, I mean? I thought it was about the American female experience – you know, what do Seven Jane Walden's hope for? Dream about? What stories do they have to tell, how do they live their lives?*

*Crap, could it be about more? Am I even asking the right questions? Can I pull off more than that? What if – just for a second, imagine it – the book could be*

*about everything: inter-connectedness, the information age (We are still in that age, right? Maybe the end of the information age? I must Google that...), femininity, masculinity, even? Should I focus on relationships? Nope. I don't have one of those, remember. My Gabriel Oak is waiting for me back in Cali, waiting for me to make him into the man he's supposed to be. Or something like that.*

*Of course, then there's Christian. Sweet, sweet Christian. Poor guy. I don't think the trip is going well for him. He sold nothing in Nebraska. "We are the Knights of NE, and we don't want your beer, now go away." No Jane, you can't make fun. this is serious. I need to be there for Christian. I must find a way to help him, since he's helping me so much. Oh, that gives me an idea. I think I'll plan a surprise for him. I'm thinking it over now, and this surprise could be huge. Can I pull it off? Yes, I will, for Christian.*

\* \* \*

That morning, Peter was already at work, so they said a nice goodbye to Mom Jane and adorable Wyatt. He seemed sad at first, and wanted Christian to play. Then he suddenly seemed okay and hugged them both goodbye. *How quickly the young adapt.* Jane tickled him one last time, then they got on the road.

It was nearly a twelve-hour drive from Nebraska to their next stop in Manitowoc, Wisconsin. Six hours in, Jane had taken over driving. Christian was reluctant, but he said that he hadn't slept well the night before, so he could use a nap. Jane was surprised, since she had slept like the proverbial rock. He had rushed off to the bathroom early, bounding out of bead, almost panicked. He was fully dressed when he came out of the bathroom. It was odd behavior, but she had bigger things to think about.

Jane noticed Christian had woken in the passenger seat and was silently grabbing at his phone, scrolling and poking. Jane enjoyed driving. Although the GPS had been a little glitchy. Almost as if her tone of voice was a little sharp. Jane would have to remind Christian to do an update when they got home.

Jane gave a chipper, "Hey, sleepy head. Good afternoon. Actually, nearly good evening."

"Hey." Christian raised his glasses, squinting, as though they'd suddenly stopped working.

"Still tired?"

"Hmm," Christian offered.

Jane countered, "Hmm yourself. I don't think I like grumpy Christian."

"Sorry. Just distracted. Weird dreams. I'm good." He continued scrolling on his phone.

"Okay, short sentence man. We should be in Manitowoc in the next hour. I hope I'm saying that right. Man-it-ow-oc. You made the reservation at the hotel, right?"

"Yep. It's only two stars, but we need to economize, especially since we still have Massachusetts and New York coming up. We really should try to just spend the day in Massachusetts. Hotels are out-rageous there."

"No, no. We are staying in two-stars now, so we can splurge in the two greatest cities in the world. Don't take that away from me." warned Jane.

"Yeah, well. I actually already paid for the hotel in New York, so we're good there. We'll figure out Mass. when we get closer." He sighed, "If I don't sell any beer her in Wisconsin, we'll be homeless, wandering around Central Park."

"Oooh! Central Park. I can't wait."

"Well, you'll have to. We have Wisconsin Jane and Massachusetts Jane to get through first. Did you con-firm with both of them, my flighty California Jane?"

"Hey! Watch it buster. I am getting my shit to-gether. We are on a mission. This book is going to be huge!"

"And I believe in you 1000%. If that was possible, but it's not. There can only be 100% of anything. I know that's a controversial statement. I have had epic battles online about it. But I have spoken. I be-lieve in you exactly 100%, Jane."

"Thank you, good sir. Okay – recap. So far, I've had the all-business-Vegas-Jane and the Mom-wife-nice-Jane. Both nice people, but not super interesting yet. I need some drama."

"I thought that was Jane number seven." Chris-tian's smile returned.

"You mean me? Funny. I see what you did there." She considered the remark. "Wait, do you really think I'm a Drama Queen?"

"I wouldn't say that. Maybe a Drama Princess. You seem to need a few things going wrong to feel... I don't know. Normal?"

"You are losing merit points fast." Banter aside, she wanted to know, "I didn't know you thought that. Give me an example."

"Well, your sister. You don't like that she judges you. You end up fighting with her at family things. But, she's actually kind of funny. She has the same sense of humor as you. And, you judge people as much as she does."

"I do not!"

"Really?" Christian did his arched eyebrow thing. "We literally sit on benches at theme parks and judge people as they walk by."

Jane laughed, "That's true. That's my favorite part, actually."

"Right. With your sister, it feels like you need some drama there – like you have to steer it into some kind of 'story construct.' "

"Wow. Pretty deep for a Lit major."

"I started out as business major, remember. I switched sophomore year. Lots of psychology in both, by the way."

"I keep forgetting that."

Christian adjusted his glasses. "My point is, I wish you could see your sister for who she is, instead of who you think she has to be in relation to you."

"What I'm hearing is that you are hot for my sister."

"Holy crap. You ruined it. I'm not hot..."

"Cause it sounds like you want to jump my sister…"

"How could you even… that's not…"

"Guys in the throes of passion often lose their words. Just breathe," Jane breathed exaggeratedly as an example.

"Jane…"

"Breathe."

"I hate you," he poked Jane in the side.

"Hey. Not when I'm driving!"

"Someday you'll get it."

"Yeah, yeah. Maybe I will. I'm a writer, Christian. I create stories. You may have a point that I cast people in my life to fit a certain construct. I guess I can see that."

"Aha!" He shouted victoriously.

"But, my sister can be a bitch. I'm going to call her out when she treats me like crap. That's called being a strong woman, young Mr. Christian."

"Okay. I just hope you can clean that filter and see people more clearly."

"I see it now." Jane turned to Christian. "You. You *do* want to bone my sister. You dog!" Jane howled like a dog, turning back to face the road.

Christian just shook his head and jabbed her in the ticklish part of her ribs.

"Driving! You know, I wish you *had* got with my sister. I like her husband, don't get me wrong. John is a great guy, but then you could have been an official part of the Walden clan."

"Not my type. Plus, I wouldn't want to mess with John. He's a very large policeman. He can have her."

"Very big of you."

The GPS spoke, "Thirteen miles until destination...." Fate wondered what it was like to only have one sister. She had two, but she never saw them much. The GPS spoke, "...Please follow highlighted route."

* * *

They arrived at a two-star hotel in Manitowoc, Wisconsin around 8 o'clock that night. Christian had called ahead to tell them they would be a late check-in, and double checked that there were two beds in the room.

As they were getting out Jane said, "I just had the strangest urge to make up a story that we're married."

"Why?" Christian hefted their bags.

"You know, the way they did in old movies?"

"Well, our story is a very modern tale. Google searches, GPS, smart phones. Also, they don't care." Christian looked at the hotel, "Besides, they probably get a lot of guests that stay just an hour."

"Saucy." Jane examined the hotel, "We couldn't get anything better?"

"We could, but we are on a shoestring budget."

"As long as there are no cockroaches."

"Amen to that."

"Jewish men say amen?"

"They do, I think." Christian pointed out. "Still not Jewish, though."

Jane just smiled.

The desk clerk didn't take notice of their marital status, or much else. The only thing the young clerk was interested in was her phone, which she checked every thirty seconds. She finally handed over the two key cards. Jane got the free wi-fi password out of the clerk, who seemed strangely reluctant to hand it over. Maybe she didn't want to share the band-width that her own phone's internet was using.

After more than eleven hours on the road, they were both tired. There was talk of a movie, but Christian nixed that due to budget. They both got ready for bed, and Jane finalized the location with Jane Three at 11am the next day. Christian double checked the five stops he was to make while Jane was with her interviewee. They were both asleep instantly.

* * *

Christian woke up to a beam of strong sunlight across his face. "Shit!" he exclaimed. "Jane! wake up. It's 10:37."

Jane only stirred in her bed.

"Jane!"

She bolted up in bed, "Todd? I mean, Christian, what's wrong?"

"Todd, really?"

"Sorry! I was having a very steamy dream." she admitted groggily.

"Spare me the details." Christian rushed around the room. It's 10:37... no, 38. Your Jane is at 11, right?"

"Shit. Yes, she is! We slept for more than 12 hours?"

"Apparently. My alarm didn't go off. Neither did yours."

"I don't set mine anymore. I have you. Shit!"

They scrambled to the bathroom. Showers were out of the question, so they used the single vanity to put on deodorant and brush their teeth. It was 10:58 when Christian said, "Jane it's nearly 11. I've got everything packed. We just have to get it to the car."

"Almost done. I promise."

Christian checked his phone for the time again, "I'll go to the office and check out."

He left the room. Jane was getting the suitcases when Christian came back and banged on the door. Jane was so startled she dropped the bag. Opening the door, she said "What the hell?"

"Sorry. I'm just pissed off. Let's get going." They walked to the car as Christian explained, "Check out is at 11. I got there at 11:02. So, the very officious *Manager* explained the policy that I would have to pay for another day."

"What?" Jane yelled. "That's ridiculous!"

"Right? I know." He slammed the bags into the car. "We'll just stay here again tonight."

"No way. I, well… they charged my card already. But, we can't stay here again."

"Why not?" asked Jane.

Christian reluctantly admitted, "I may have said some unkind things about his toupee, and his general mental state."

"What?" She was surprised at very un-Christian-like behavior. "Did we just get charged for two nights, and get kicked out?"

They finished loading the bags. "I insinuated he kicks puppies, too."

"Christian!"

"Sorry. I just... let's just go." he checked the time on his phone. "Maybe we can salvage the day."

She got in the passenger seat. "Remind me not to make you mad."

They drove to the restaurant aptly named Manitowoc Coffee where Jane Three agreed to meet. She had answered the Facebook message from Our Jane in real time as she typed furiously on the way over, dripping with apologies.

Christian had called his first appointment, explaining he would be late. He dropped her off, and she made her way into the Manitowoc Coffee. It was very busy at 11:17, and obviously a small, family run restaurant with a warm, homey feel.

The middle-aged waitress asked, "Hey, hon, how many today?"

"Oh, actually I'm meeting someone." Jane scanned the room, but Jane Three had a blurry family picture for her profile pic. Not much help there.

"Are you Jane?" the waitress beamed a bright smile.

"Yeah. I mean yes, I'm meeting... *another* Jane."

"Oh yes, Jane Walden. I mean, our Jane told us all about it. Right this way." The middle-aged woman led her to the back of the dining room, where a large oval cushioned booth was populated by Jane Three, herself a middle-aged woman of 45 (according to Facebook). She wore her hair to the shoulder, woven with silver streaks. Her skin was that of a woman who worked hard, long hours and took no shit from anyone. Her build was small, but stout. Jane resisted the urge to think her man-ish, because she was all woman somehow despite the gruff exterior. A man about her age sat in the booth, with thinning brown hair which left only a crow's nest around his head. He was a slender man, but had a protruding beer belly. They were not sitting next to each other. There were also two teenagers: a pretty girl with dark hair, and a tall boy of about sixteen. She couldn't think of her as Mom Jane, that was taken. Our Jane would figure it out as she went.

"You made it." said Jane Three. This wasn't an exclamation, and it felt to our Jane like a sneer.

Our Jane pulled her notebook from her purse. "Yes. I'm so, so sorry I'm late. I don't know what could have happened to the alarm. I never sleep this late. Must be all the traveling. Anyway, no excuse. I'm so sorry. Thank you for agreeing to meet with me." Jane sat at the edge of the booth, next to the teenaged boy. The two Janes were directly across the table form each other.

"What can I get for you?" a new waitress startled Our Jane.

"Oh! Umm, nothing, thank you. Maybe a glass of water?"

Jane Three slapped the table hard with her palm. Only our Jane jumped at the startling motion. Apparently, the family was not easily startled. "You're not going to eat with us? This is a family meal I invited you to. You're not even going to break bread?"

Our Jane lost any color she'd had. She didn't know how to respond, and looked at the other Jane for a hint that she was joking. Wisconsin Jane's face was made of stone.

"Uh, I'll... I'll have a coffee, please. And an English muffin."

A hand came down flat on the table again. Our Jane jumped a second time. "Ha! I was only kidding. You are a jumpy Jane!" Jane Three let out a raspy laugh. "You should have seen your face!" *Maybe this one is Scary Jane?* She dismissed the idea.

Even the teenagers were laughing now, along with a few people at other tables.

Jane Three laughed long and loud. "Sorry, I've got a hard sense of humor. Really, I'm excited. I've been waiting all week for this. I've told anyone that will listen that I'm being interviewed for a book! You made me a local celebrity, at least for a few minutes. Sorry if I scared you. Let's make it official. Jane Walden. Nice to meet you." She stood up the best she could and offered her hand to our Jane across the table.

She shook it and was surprised at the masculine firmness of the shake. Wisconsin Jane explained, "Dad always told us only a firm handshake will do."

"I'm the one that's sorry. So rude to be late, and thank you for letting me meet your family."

"Speaking of that, the guy to your right is Tony Junior, this is my daughter Elizabeth. I'm practicing not calling her Lizzie."

"Mom!" said Elizabeth, turning the shade of embarrassed teen.

"I'm getting better, Elizabeth. And this is Tony Senior. Speaking of that, you got me just in time. After the divorce is final, I'm going back to my maiden name. I won't be Jane Walden much longer. Hope that doesn't disqualify me."

Jane looked around the table. The teenagers looked uncomfortable, but resigned. Joe Senior just continued eating.

"I'm... I'm so sorry. I had no idea. When I saw you all as a family, the photos on Facebook, I assumed..."

"It's alright. We've been split up for a few years now, saving up for the divorce." explained Jane Three. "The paperwork is filed now, finally, and we're just waiting for the written decree from the judge."

"Wow, I better write this down." She'd brought along many spiral notebooks with her, and was dismayed when she opened it to reveal blank pages, none of the Jane questionnaire she'd been toying with.

"Sh... I mean, crap. I brought the wrong notebook."

"What do you mean?" asked Jane Three, crunching some white toast.

"No notes. I brought an empty notebook... never mind. I'll just wing it. Sorry, let me just write some notes." She scribbled for a few seconds: divorce, no longer Walden. "Is it okay to ask questions about the divorce? Is that too much?"

"You're the writer. I'm not shy." Jane Three laughed. "obviously."

Tony Senior made a non-committal grunt. Jane Three shot him a warning glance.

"If you're getting divorced, why are you having a family meal? Isn't that, well, kind of odd?"

Jane pointed to her son, "Junior, you know the rule. No phones at meals."

Tony Junior put down his phone on the booth next to him. Jane noticed it was still where he could see it. Junior said, "We're an odd family."

Jane smiled at his delivery, not just his words. Lots of subtext there, and Jane noticed a silent agreement on the face of his sister Elizabeth.

"We're still a family. Tony is still the father of these two. That won't change even though he cheated on me," said Jane Three. Our Jane noticed the daughter roll her eyes. "Being a dumbass doesn't take away the title of father."

Tony Senior only shook his head at that, almost imperceptible, but Our Jane noticed. There was a family dynamic at work Jane needed to understand.

"We've had our big blow-out fights a long time ago. I'm getting more hours at the company. Sorry, we live in Manitowoc – we all just call it *The Company*. Anyway, dumbass here is giving me the house. He's already started to move out, little by little. We're

102

adults. The marriage is over, we move on," Jane Three finished.

*That's it – this one is Iron Jane. Tough as Iron.*

"Wow, that's very... I don't know, grounded of you. I'm not sure I could be friends with my ex. Even live together after a break-up." She thought of Todd, and the steamy dream. She also remembered his constant cheating, and eyed Tony Senior differently.

Iron Jane elaborated, "You know, it's hard. Tony is a good father, always has been. We try to be as reasonable as possible. You can go around with your pain on your sleeve, but at the end of the day, you still have to do the dishes, you know? You still gotta to go to work to put food on the table. I mean, look at Junior. He's over six foot and still growing. Eats like a frickin' horse. When his friends come over, forget it."

Jane made more notes, and took a bite of her English muffin which had arrived promptly. "I could talk about just this part of your life, it's so interesting."

"Yeah? Are you really going to put this stuff in a book? How does that even work? Do you need me to sign some sort of paper or something?"

Jane's worries blossomed again. "A release form? I haven't got that far yet. I'm still in the interview and research phase."

"Really? I figured you'd have your ducks all in a row, with driving clear across country and all."

"Yeah. This trip happened kind of fast. I thought if you met with me, that would be like permission." Jane made a note and underlined it. "I'll have to research that."

"Can't you just ask your publisher? I'm sure they have a department that handles that. They probably have standard forms. I know our legal and HR sure do. Three forms for everything!"

"I don't... I mean I'm still sending out book proposals." *I must find a faster way to explain this. Or just get my shit together*, thought Jane. She said, "The way it works is I send book proposals to literary agents, they accept it. I write the book, then my agent sells it to a publishing house."

A laugh exploded out of Iron Jane. "Wait, you mean, you don't know if anyone will ever publish your book? The way you said over Facebook, made me think this was a done deal."

"Well, well, it will be!" Our Jane blurted, "I mean, you know, the idea is so good, so marketable that, of course an agent's going to sell it."

Iron Jane put up her hand. "I meant no offense." She was still laughing, "I'll sign any form you need, or you can just use anything I say. I'm just a little surprised. Your plan just seems a little..."

"Shaky." Tony Senior spoke for the first time. He looked in her eyes, "You might want to think this through a little better. Ever heard of Joe Frank?"

"No." Jane felt like her idea was under assault. Her tone came out edgy. "Who's Joe Frank?"

Tony Senior replied, "He's this radio guy. He started on NPR years ago. Anyway, one of his shows was 'Joe Frank's America' – called up all these other Joe Franks across the country and interviewed them on air. I figured that's where your idea came from. Might want to check it out."

Jane couldn't find words. Her first instinct was to curl up into a ball. Had she stolen someone's idea? She scanned her memory for any "Joe Frank." She listened to NPR in her car sometimes. Anger rose in her, but it was quickly overtaken by a nauseating wave of doubt. She stood up on shaky legs. "Excuse me, please, I need to use the restroom."

The family exchanged glances that only their Walden clan understood.

She found the small restroom, noting how clean it was before she splashed cold water on her face. She sat on the toilet, lid down. She'd never had an actual panic attack, but she noted with alarm that her hands shook. She sat there, maybe five minutes, then felt better. *This is a good idea. I didn't steal it. I will write this book.*

She got back to the table, and only Iron Jane remained, putting on her coat. "Tony took the kids home. We have separate cars. I need a cigarette. Want to join me?"

Jane hadn't smoked since high school, and then only briefly. When they got outside, Jane handed Jane a cigarette and lit it for her. After an initial coughing fit, Jane remembered why she smoked in high school. The doubt drifted away with the tendrils of smoke. "This is exactly what I needed. Thank you."

"I keep trying to quit these things. I'm down to three smokes a day. My latest excuse has been the divorce, but since I'm kicking him out, I guess I have to invent another."

"I'm sorry I seemed so unprepared today. I'm usually a lot more organized. Can I contact you with follow up questions, since I screwed today up so badly?"

"Of course." Iron Jane released a long line of smoke. "I'll wrote down my cell for you. Now that I've met you and know you're not a crazy person, here you go. Call me anytime. In the back of my mind I had all these ideas that you were an identity thief, or something like that. But you didn't ask for my blood type or social security number." Iron Jane finished with a smoky laugh.

"Yeah, I mean yes. Thanks for that. I can't believe I'm so scattered."

Iron Jane consoled her. "Well, it's a big thing to write a book. I wouldn't even know how to begin. I love to read, but writing seems like, I don't know, magic."

"You're right, it does feel like magic sometimes. I'm glad I'm getting back to it." Our Jane felt a need to explain, "My job got in the way, life, etcetera. But now, I'm focused. I just don't know if I fully understand how big this idea could be… if I do it right, that is. Thank your husband for the Joe Frank thing. And thank you for the cigarette, I'm glad Christian didn't see me."

"Oh, Christian, is it? Like that dirty book? What, Grey something? He's your guy, then?"

Our Jane laughed. "No, no. Nothing like that. He's my best friend. He's along for the ride with this book adventure."

"Good looking?" asked Iron Jane, taking a puff.

"Christian? I suppose, if you like the millennial type."

Iron Jane wrinkled her brow. "What type is that?"

"Clean cut, nice, considerate, not particularly muscular."

Iron Jane laughed, "Would he agree with this description?"

"Probably. Then he'd add a few more qualities to the list. He is super smart."

"What's your type, then?"

"Oh, Broad shoulders, hot guys that are messed up. Think Mel Gibson in Lethal Weapon."

"Wasn't he suicidal in that?"

"Okay, not that messed up. But 1980's movie stars seem to be exactly my type. Or a burly nineteenth century sheep herder." Our Jane puffed wistfully, "I'm living in the wrong era."

Iron Jane rubbed her cigarette butt into the blacktop parking lot. "Setting your expectations pretty high, Miss Jane Walden."

"Impossibly high, I'm sure," Our Jane extinguished her own cigarette. "Thanks for doing this. Really. I'll have more questions..."

"When you get your shit together?" Iron Jane smiled. "Come on, a hand shake won't do it." She hugged Our Jane, laughing the deep smokers laugh. They said their goodbyes and Iron Jane walked to her car. Our Jane felt the wave of doubt saturate her mind again, the buzz from the cigarette fading too quickly. She tapped on her phone to search for this mysterious Joe Frank.

Then Jane looked up, and was startled to realize she was right next to the ocean. She quickly dismissed the idea, vaguely remembering her geography, and realized it must be a Great Lake. She was inwardly embarrassed to realize she didn't know at which great lake she was staring. Jane walked to the barrier overlooking the great body of water. Her phone told her it was Lake Michigan. Living in California, she knew the oceans, and had been to many lakes of various sizes.

The Great Lake Michigan looked like the sea. There was a marina with familiar looking boats of all types. Looking at the horizon, she could not see past the other side, just like the horizon over the sea. It looked the same. The waves breaking on the shore were smaller than ocean waves, then she suddenly realized the main difference. She sniffed the air.

The smell. It was the smell that was different, maybe the reason she hadn't noticed it at all. No briny, salty smell. It was an odd sensation. It was like tasting cherry when you were expecting watermelon. Now she looked out to the immensity of the Great Lake, and another thought came.

These were still, deep waters, as deep as many oceans. Jane suddenly felt like she was at sea. She was still embarrassed how unprepared she felt. Now a new doubt about the originality of her idea rolled around her head, making her dizzy. She sat on a bench, facing the great Lake Michigan. Her spiral notebook on her lap, she began making notes, realizing that if she wasn't careful, she might get swallowed by the deep waters of her own idea.

Christian came back to pick her up at around 1:30. He was smiling. "Wisconsin loves their micro-brews. Two out of three distributors ordered stock. 100 cases total commitment. Wait, what's wrong?"

"I don't think I can do this, Christian."

Christian's smile faltered. "What? What happened?"

"I haven't thought this through! There is so much that I haven't... I don't know why I thought I could do this!"

"Hey, hey. Hang on there. You're doing fine. It's a big thing you're doing, okay. But it's a good idea. *I* want to read the book you are going to write. What happened with this Jane?"

"Actually, she was kind of cool; tough, blunt, an Iron Jane. She's has this big personality, an interesting story with the divorce and all."

"She's getting divorced? That sucks."

"But it's interesting too. She won't be a Jane Walden anymore, it's her married name. They're still living in the same house. The kids seem strangely well-adjusted. But I go and muck it up when I'm late and I bring the wrong notebook." She held up the notebook, "No notes. I felt naked."

"Crap. I knew you shouldn't have brought two red notebooks. You just winged it?"

"Yeah, and I've got her number now, so I can do follow up." She pointed at Lake Michigan as though Christian would automatically get the simile. "I just feel overwhelmed. Can I really do this?"

"Yes, you can, because I just sold 100 cases! Things are looking up for both of us." Christian rallied Jane. "Now, I'm taking you to a pub, we'll get some food, a beer, then dessert."

"Wow. Big spender."

"The dessert is so we can sober up, because right after, we hit the road for Massachusetts. We have to haul butt to make it for Jane number four. It's 1100 miles."

"Oh crap, that's right. How long is that?"

"Straight through, 18 hours." Christian said, "It's a long haul. Let's go celebrate before we have to leave."

Jane perked up. "Beer, and food that's bad for us?"

"You know it." said Christian. "I want to take you to this cool pub a distributor told me about."

Jane smiled. *You saved me again, kid.*

On the way, Jane called up "Joe Frank's America" on her phone. It was just under 30 minutes: A montage of interviews from other Joe Franks all over America. Young, old, all walks of life. It aired in 1996 and right in the middle, features a voice over from the radio star Joe Frank. The peculiar thing is that he admits the idea freaked him out. He said he had to take constant breaks. In fact, it even made him question if he wanted to retire from the radio business. Toward the end a ghostly version of the song "Me and My Shadow" is interwoven.

"That was really cool. I wonder if he was really depressed, or if it was kind of performance art?" said Christian.

"Cool? It was awesome. Shit!" Jane wanted Christian to rise to the new emotional crisis. *Why is he so calm?* "So that's it, my idea is not original at all."

"I disagree. This was recorded in 1996. He was dialing people up out of phone books on a landline phone. Before the internet took hold, before social media. Your story, even the basis of the idea, is totally fresh."

Jane kept quiet for a few minutes, finally admitting, "Okay. Maybe you're right." An idea clicked, "Hey! What if I include this Joe Frank guy in the book, integrate it as part of the narrative. Would that be enough?"

"You mean, give a nod to the idea he had? Even though the ideas are only slightly connected? Great idea. That should do it."

"Okay. Thank God. Crisis averted." She wondered if Christian smelled the smoke on her. She didn't volunteer the smoky chat she had with Iron Jane. "This definitely calls for beer."

Christian smiled. "As you wish, my lady. There it is."

The Law House Pub was a brightly lit, modern looking space in a building with obvious history. Jane eyed the primarily brick building, "Is it called that because a lot of lawyers come here?"

"That's what the guy told me. He said the courthouse is across the street, sheriff's office a block away. Makes sense, I guess."

She spotted the band, "Oh, live music? I like, I like."

It was a three-piece band set up in a corner of the pub. No stage, just on the hardwood floor. A man and woman were up front, with guitars and mics, the drummer cozily tucked in behind.

Jane couldn't tell their ages, exactly, although the impression was late thirties or maybe early forties. The woman had long hair in a ponytail and seemed timeless, like a woman who looked 25, but was happy to tell you she was 50 with grown children. She was rocking the bass guitar on a rousing rendition of "Mustang Sally." The male singer wore a fisherman's low cap, that Jane always associated with Irishmen for a reason she never understood.

He was keeping them in suspense holding the note. "One of these early mornins', yeah. Woow! Gonna be wipin' yo weepin' eyes. H'uh!

It was just three pm, the beginning of happy hour, and Jane was sorry to see only four tables were occupied. The small crowd cheered like a full house as the song came to an end.

"Thank you, ladies and gents. We are The Sally John Trio, and we are taking our first little break. Grab some grub and a *brew*. We'll be back shortly to *you*. See what I did there?"

Jane laughed. Rhyming puns in a pub; Christian had found the right spot. They grabbed a seat and flipped through the laminated happy hour menu on the table.

A server showed up quickly, "Hey folks. My name is Eric. I'll be your server. can I start you with a flight of micro-brews?"

"Yes please!" announced Jane. Decision made.

"Jane. We have to get on the road before too long. One beer, remember? Two tops."

"Okay. Dad. Unless…" she leaned provocatively into Christian, "You take first shift driving, then I could sleep for a while."

He eyed her suspiciously. "Okay. We are in Wisconsin. It's probably a law that we must drink beer before we leave. A flight for the lady. And I have my eye on the Brenner Brewing Bacon Bomb. And regular menus, please."

"Nice choice – Wisconsin brand. Cheese curds to start?" asked professional up-seller Eric.

"What is that, exactly?" asked Jane, skeptically.

Eric raised an eyebrow.

Christian nodded. He told Jane, "The guy I talked to said we had to try them – Wisconsin must." Back to Eric, he said, "we're from California, dude. They would probably make them out of tofu back home."

Eric smiled. Jane shrugged. "When in Rome, right? Please bring on the cheese curds, Eric."

Eric left with a smile. Jane said, "look at you, Mr. Considerate. Always using first names and such. You are a good man, Christian Jacobsen."

"I know, I know. Also, stunning in the sack. And modest, of course."

"True to the modest part. Stop trying to get me to imagine you having sex."

He steered to another topic, "What's the next Jane like? Massachusetts Jane - Number Four?"

"Jane Four. Yeah, that's easier than saying Massachusetts all the time. Well..." Jane got out her phone to refresh her memory. She snapped a quick shot of her and Christian. "She's a year younger than me. Her Facebook photos are kinda wild and fun. She definitely likes to party. But she's sporadic with her posting. She had quite a few heartfelt, seriously inappropriate tweets on twitter. Mostly political."

"Well, it is Massachusetts, a Revolution started there. I'm sure strong opinions abound."

"I even agree with some of them, but wow. Some are over the top. She's not the 'soul of tact,'" Jane accentuated the last phrase with an upper crust, east coast accent.

"Does she leave *wicked* remarks? Talk about parking in *Harva'd ya'd.*"

"That was both cliché and a terrible Boston accent. I know very little about Massachusetts, Mr. History Buff, so you'll have to help me in my research. This Jane looks like a scrappy kid. Should be a lot of material there."

The beers arrived, and they were handed menus. The drink flight consisted of six small glasses of beer, each with a few ounces, going from left to right, lightest to darkest. They both sipped their beers while looking at the menu. There were cleverly titled categories like "pre-trial motion, cross examination, Judge's rule."

Christian ordered a burger, Jane got a chicken dish with walnut-cranberry sauce. Then the cheese curds arrived.

"I'm dubious – just fried cheese?" Jane pulled the dish between them.

"Fried cheese curds, I think that's different. Definitely aren't cheese sticks. Batter fried with... I think this is a raspberry vinegar type dip. I'm game."

Jane shrugged. "Okay. Let's do this."

Then they both tasted them.

Jane eyes tripled in size. "Oh, my God! Where have these been all my life? I must have twelve dozen of these, stat!"

Christian felt the curd melt in his mouth, "15 dozen, at least. These are amazing."

A few more tables had filled up. The three band members had been sitting at the bar, now they began a fresh set.

"Folks, since the bigger crowd should be here soon, this is usually the time we inflict some of our own music on the patient crowd. Don't worry, it's just a couple original songs, then we'll get back to the rock and classic R & B."

Christian and Jane gave a round of applause at the idea.

"Thanks folks, we appreciate that. Hopefully you're still clapping when you hear it. You may sense a theme. I'm Johnny Jay Johnson. Yep, alliteration – I've heard all the jokes. This is my wife and killer bass player Sally Ann Johnson. Behind us is my brother, Powerhouse Pete. This one's called Sally Ann. I think you can probably guess why."

> *Sally Ann*
> *You're getting attention again*
> *Yes, I think of you now and then*
> *And I'd take the chance to dance with*
> *Sally Ann*

"These guys are good," said Jane.
"They are," replied Christian, nodding with the beat.

> *You were the one and it's true*
> *Nobody could slow dance quite like you*
> *On you played, broke some hearts too*
> *And the music is playing*
> *For another fine dark romance*
> *Sally Ann.*

The food arrived. "Oooh. 'Another fine dark romance'. I like that." Jane dug into her chicken dish.

> *Listen, the songs haven't changed*
> *And I've never quite been the same*
> *Since the smoke got in our eyes*
> *Sally Ann.*

> *From the boy who stood there*
> *Though he didn't seem to care*
> *He wanted you to know he's loving you*
> *Loving you,*
> *Sally Ann.*

Christian smiled at the lyrics, and the big finish. The applause was surprising large from the small-ish crowd. Jane added a few loud whistles between bites.

Johnny Johnson said, "Thanks folks. Very kind, very kind. This next one's called Lullabies and Softer Lies."

> *Until you find the time…*
> *Don't be so inviting.*

They talked close to each other between bites. Jane shot a sideways glance at Christian. "How are you doing, kid?"

"Me? Fine." Christian narrowed his eyes. "Why do you ask?"

"You've been kinda quiet the last few days. Subdued."

> *When you tell me no*
> *Don't be so enticing*
> *If you mean to go*
> *If you don't want me*
> *It's not fair.*

"Oh, you know. Lost in thought. Worried about the business. Worried about Dad."

"Is he okay?"

"Yeah… I guess. I mean, on the surface he's okay." Christian struggled to articulate, "There seems to be an understanding, an unspoken thing that we don't go near certain subjects. I guess it's a guy thing."

> *Knowing there you'll be*
> *When I feel your touch*
> *I could drift away and dream*

"Subjects like your Mom? So that's where you get it from." Jane looked into Christian's eyes.

"Yeah," he looked away.

Jane sipped her third little beer, "You never talk to her. Does your dad?"

"No." he considered that, "not that I know of."

"Don't you think that's sad?"

> *That I am the only one*
> *You hate to leave*
> *I should walk away*
> *Never tell you what I mean*
> *So until I change my mind...*

"I think the whole thing's sad," Christian shifted in his seat. "Mostly I'm just angry at her."

"And your Dad?"

"He knows where she is of course, for mail and stuff like that. Hey, this is a really good song."

> *Lullaby's and softer lies*
> *Will not still this heart of mine*
> *There are no goodbyes*
> *For you and I*
> *No such thing as an end of time.*

It was a slower tempo, but the crowd loved it just as much.

Jane really listened to the last line. "That *was* a good song. Sorry, I didn't mean to talk over it. I'm just worried about you."

"Long Train Running" by the Doobie Brothers began and Christian was suddenly out of his chair.

"Dance with me!" Christian exclaimed, eyes glinting as he offered a hand.

Jane had just taken a bite of chicken. Before she could object, he pulled her in front of the band.

"Hey now. What the..." Jane was surprised by Christian's boldness. They used to go to the occasional club with a few friends. But that felt like ages ago. How long since she danced? Todd was not a dancer. He stomped around the dance floor when he was drunk enough, but it was no pleasure. She'd react by totally ignoring him and dancing alone.

Now she and Christian were dancing to a classic rock song. She wondered at Christian. Just an attempt to change the conversation, or a genuine attempt to cut loose? Since he'd only had one beer, it couldn't be that. But Jane had begun on her fourth sample/flight beer. It was beginning to hit. She closed her eyes and moved.

She opened them to see Christian with moves of his own. She said, "Those look like some new moves, kid."

"Maybe I've been practicing. Maybe I'm just a natural dancer." He started to get wilder and more accentuated, his movements broader.

At first, Jane though he was self-mocking with the wild moves, then she realized he could dance. Really dance. *Is this a new facet of him, one I never saw?* He grabbed her waist, swung Jane around and they were dancing with each other for real now. It felt good, especially with the alcohol hitting her senses. The song was over before she knew it and Christian took her hand and led them back to the table.

Jane saw a message waiting on her cell phone. It was the email she used just for writing correspondence. She opened it with excitement and it read:

> *"Thank you so much for your book proposal Seven Ways to Jane. I'm intrigued by the idea, though it sounds familiar. I'd like to see three sample chapters. Your book proposal is interesting, but I need to see how well you write. Looking forward to hearing from you.*
>
> *Leona Andrews*
>
> *Andrews, Dicus and Moore Literary."*

"Oh my God, oh my God!" Jane showed Christian her phone.

"That's fantastic!"

She raised a glass, "Cheers!" Jane felt a little silly slamming her tiny sample beer glass next to Christian's 22-ounce beer, now almost empty. But she didn't care. Finally, she was getting her chance.

She downed the sample beer and started on sample beer number five. She was almost done when she said, "Oh shit."

"What's wrong? This is good news, right?"

"Yes, and no. I put a book proposal together, but I haven't actually written any chapters yet!"

"Uh oh." Christian downed some more beer.

"I've been using notebooks. And occasionally making digital notes from my handwritten notes, but I haven't actually written a word. Oh my God, Christian. Oh, my God. What am I going to do?"

Christian finished the last of his beer. "We're going to get dessert like I promised, let our beer settle. I only had one, so after dessert I'll drive, and you get in that car and write like a crazy lady. You can have three chapters to send to this agent. This is all under control. College cram time. We did it then, We can do it now."

Jane was sloshing down her sixth sample beer when she waved for the server to come over.

"Umm, Eric, right? We need the dessert menu, oh – and two glasses of water."

"No worries. You guys looked good up there on the dance floor." remarked Eric.

Jane raised the last bit of her beer in a salute and the server cleared the plates before he left to get the dessert menu.

They shared dessert, which was way too filling, but it gave time for the effect of the beer to wear off. Christian was worried that Jane would be too buzzed to write a word, but after leaving the restaurant, she put her hair in a determined ponytail and got to work.

Christian programmed the GPS for the next Jane in Massachusetts, and they were on the road. Fate noticed the satisfied smiles on their faces. Alcohol perhaps? No, they seemed sober. Jane seemed determined, tapping at her laptop. Christian smiled at her. The road to New England might be intense. Fate would be working hard to keep them on track.

# Chapter 7

# On Track

"What lies behind you and what lies in front of you,
pales in comparison to what lies inside of you."
– Ralph Waldo Emerson

*QUICK JOURNAL CHECK-IN*

*Okay, the first two chapters are done. I'll have the third done within the hour. Thank God I'm a fast typist. Stopping to quickly journal, and take a little break.*

*I feel like such an idiot. Of course, I knew the next step was them asking for sample chapters. I've done all the research. But I wasn't prepared for them actually asking for any. It just makes me realize (again) that I'm less prepared than I should be. I'm getting sick of my own angst. From now on, I'm all in. No more mistakes, no more being unprepared.*

*Christian has been a rock. He's driven eight hours now and I know he must be exhausted. One more hour of writing, then I'll take the wheel.*

*I'm still hoping my surprise works out for Christian. But I must concentrate on these chapters now. Am I blowing this?*

* * *

Christian drove for nine hours, nearly half the way to Massachusetts. He only took a thirty-minute nap before he woke up and read over Jane's three chapters while she drove.

Jane tried very hard to keep her eyes on the road, and open. One time she did close her eyes, and she could swear the GPS got louder. She snapped awake immediately.

Christian loved everything her writing, but this was the most important thing she'd ever written. The most important three chapters she'd ever write, if it meant getting an agent. Jane had read that you only send your very best work to an agent. Even though you know it's going to be picked apart later. "Is it okay that this is just barely beyond a first draft?" she asked Christian.

"No, and yes. You definitely need to rewrite and polish. I typed in some notes. I used track changes, so it should be pretty easy to fix everything. But yes, this is good, Jane. Rushed, but well-written. You still got it, kid."

Those last five words warmed her. Christian stared straight out. Again Jane tried not to look at him, focusing on the road. She finally asked, "Hmm. There is a very big '*but*' coming – isn't there?"

"Well, I read over your proposal again, and then compared that with these three chapters. They're technically correct; the three chapters follow your proposal. But I think you're right, the book is about more."

Jane stared ahead, her hands fluttered nervously on the steering wheel.

Christian wanted to be nothing but supportive and knew he had to find the right words, "Your proposal says the book is about connecting in the information age with people that are like you in one way, but totally different from you in every other way. It says it's about universal connectivity and finding ways to open a dialogue between people that are joined together in one simple way, their name. That's good. But it almost sounds like a scientific paper."

"Well. Okay. Poop." His assessment hit her square in the spot that was bothering her. "I know there is something missing, I just can't figure out what."

Christian said, "I don't think it's fair to tell you what I think it should be about."

"What? Why not? Please tell me if you know. You can't hold back on shit like that!"

"At the risk of doing the very thing that I said I didn't want to do - That's just it. I think this is a about a journey of self-discovery. I mean it's called ego surfing for a reason. You type in your name because it started with ego. But, do people want to read a book about a millennial girl flitting around America looking at different versions of herself? Is that self-aware enough? In a way, I think it needs to be more about you. In a non-egotistical way, but I think you need to examine how this journey is changing you. This is what I see. Sorry if it doesn't help you exactly."

She turned his opinion over in her mind. "A journey of self-discovery."

"Yes. But I think it's a more than that."

The GPS told Jane to keep on course, as the road curved up ahead. Fate tried to keep the irony out of her voice, considering their conversation.

"Ugg! Christian! What is it? What am I missing?"

"I think you need to open yourself up; see more of what you're experiencing. See a little deeper. Okay, that sounds pretentious. But it seems like you are so preoccupied with getting the right questions to the other Janes - or getting the right unique nickname for each different Jane, that you might be missing details. The story needs to sing. Right now, it's merely humming a catchy tune. This needs to be kind of the lyrical nonfiction. Your writing talent is worthy of a deeper dive. Just open yourself up more. I know you'll find it."

"Okay, okay." the practical kept yelling in her brain. "But I need to send the first three chapters back as soon as possible. A delay may be a red flag to the agent."

The GPS told her politely to keep East on I-90. Fate thought of the dangers of sending sample chapters to prospective agents without them being polished. She grasped how many automatic fails there were in the query and submission process and worried how many landmines Jane had written for herself.

"Listen," Christian soothed, "we still have over eight hours of driving. Let's switch. I can drive some more while you polish."

"Christian, you must be exhausted. Go back to sleep and wake up in four hours. I'll be fine. Worry will keep me awake, trust me."

Christian hesitated. "Okay. I really could use the sleep. Two hours, tops. Then I'll take back over and you should have those chapters polished and ready to go by the time we get to Massachusetts. You said you were having trouble with the Massachusetts version of you. Any word?"

"Yeah, she says she's getting a new phone. I've only talked with her through Facebook Messenger and Twitter... Oh, hey. Speak of the devil and she will appear." Jane handed her phone to Christian. A new message had popped up. "That's Jane Four now. Can you check the Facebook message and tell me what she says? The password is..."

"Got it." Christian was already into her phone and checking the bubble-style message. "You've had the same password forever, despite the parade of phones you've gone through. She writes 'Hey sister Jane. Had to use my friend's laptop. Got all the messages, and it sounds cool. Having trouble getting that phone, so I'll be waiting at the Pond on the 23rd around 11 am. Cool?'"

Jane dictated, "Tell her cool. See you then."

Christian typed, then put the phone in the cup holder between them. "Done. Hope she shows. Who doesn't have a phone these days? How does she live? And, you know, watch cat videos?"

"I know, right? She may end up being the flighty Jane, so I can give up my crown. I kind of hope she is. Now, you sir, go to sleep. I'll wake you up in two hours."

Christian closed Jane's laptop to preserve battery power and put in the backseat carefully. He then took his pillow and put it against the window. He was out within seconds.

The GPS kept giving Jane clear directions, and Jane used every trick she could think of to stay awake. She pinched herself, she got coffee when stopping for gas. Christian was still out, so she didn't even ask if he wanted anything. Jane tried different breathing techniques, taping her fingers, everything. Just as she thought she was going to nod off, her smartphone alarm went off. It was time to wake Christian up and switch.

They were several hours outside of the spot where they told the other Jane to meet. Jane wondered how she smelled. They'd been a long time in the car and Jane decided to do the switch off at a gas station. Hopefully the bathroom she'd tidy up in wouldn't be too gross.

They were to meet Jane Four around 11 am. It was just before seven in the morning when Jane checked her phone clock. The sun had just risen. Christian woke and was surprised to see that it was no longer dark. He roused himself quickly.

128

"Service station. Good idea. I'll start filling up when you go to the bathroom. I'll get some coffee and get my tooth paste and stuff."

"Sounds like a plan." She got her toiletry bag and made her way to the restroom. She had to go inside to get the key which was attached to a ridiculously large piece of wood painted bright orange. The lack of sleep and the absurd orange-ness made her giggle.

Christian was true to his organization skills and by the time Jane got to the bathroom he'd bought his coffee, the car was gassed up, the nozzle replaced, and he stood just outside the door waiting for her.

"Is that the *Bottega Veneta*?" Christian sniffed as she walked by him.

Perplexity swam across Jane's face. "You know what perfume I'm wearing?"

"I guessed." Christian shrugged. "That's the expensive one your Dad bought for you last year, right?"

"Yeah." Jane surveyed him up and down. She shook her head, "You're really weird about some things, you know?"

"I know." he agreed with a groggy nod.

Christian shrugged and went to the bathroom. Like most guys, he was in and out of the bathroom in about ten minutes. Often Jane was very jealous of men and their speedy clean-up powers. Then she remembered how hairy some of their backs were, and changed her opinion. Good to be a girl, she reaffirmed. She shared her decision aloud, "Nope, I wouldn't want to be a guy."

"Were we discussing a subject that I'm not a part of?"

"Kind of. I was just momentarily jealous of how fast guys get ready in the morning. Mind you, I wouldn't miss *not* having periods. But who wants to deal with one of those floppy things all day?" she vaguely waved at his crotch area. "It's like having a Mr. Snuffleupagus from Sesame Street between your legs. No thanks."

"Are you sure?" Christian examined his own body. "No babies come out of us, either. And we get to pee standing up. It's pretty awesome."

"Maybe. But I've smelled guys' bathrooms before. You all seem to miss a lot."

"Not my bathroom, thank you. I aim with a lot of care. Yeah, penises come with a set of issues… but nothing like vaginas. Those things are a nightmare. Besides, when you have a giant firehose like mine…"

"Gross! I did not want an image of your penis in my head, thank you. New subject, you sure you're okay to drive the last few hours? I really want to polish these chapters and send them out."

"Polish away. I've got my coffee, so I'm good. But make sure you get some sleep before the next Jane."

"I'm good. It's all about the work now. Maybe I'll figure out what's missing before I meet the next Jane."

Christian smiled. He knew she would figure it all out.

As they buckled up, Fate smiled to herself conspiratorially, and willed them both to stay on course.

# Chapter 8

# Walden

"It's not what you look at that matters, it's what you see."
– Henry David Thoreau

They arrived to meet Jane Four at 11:09 a.m.

Walden Pond, surrounded by Walden Woods is a naturally beautiful area which inspired Henry David Thoreau to write many books: *Walden*, among others. He lived there between 1845 and 1847. He's widely acclaimed as one of the grandfathers of the modern ecological movement to preserve beautiful places. Jane thought it was the perfect place to meet the other Jane Walden. What she didn't know was how complicated it was to get inside the park.

"On the map it looks like I'll have to drop you inside the park and pay the fee. It'll be just as easy for you guys to walk back out. If you wouldn't mind, it'd be nice not paying that fee twice. My appointments should take about an hour and a half, then I'll come back and pick you up outside the park. That enough time?"

"I think so. She said she'd meet me in the visitor center. Oh, I think that's it over there."

There were plenty of places to park and Christian only had to stop for a moment to let Jane out. Jane made sure she had the correct red notebook. Christian left her to face Jane Four.

The visitor center was a rustic structure, but obviously on the newer side. The research she'd done online said that the musician Don Henley and his organization had funded the visitor center. A modern facility among all the nature, somehow it seemed to fit the environment. She walked up to the building, which was an open floor plan design with gift shop and offices. She peered around. It was no challenge to spot Jane Four. She seemed to change her hairstyle and look quite often, according to her social media, so she spotted the only candidate across the room.

She had blue streaks in her hair and dressed in a colorful oversized jacket. It was pink and orange and hard to miss. She made her way to the girl. Jane Four was an inch shorter than Our Jane, very pretty, but under a lot of make-up. Perhaps this Jane didn't know how pretty she was, thought she needed to distract with plumage of one sort or another. Our Jane reminded herself not to judge too quickly, and called out, "Jane? Jane Walden?"

The girl jerked, surprised. She smiled immediately. "Are you the other Jane Walden?"

This question struck her strangely. She had thought of the Janes besides herself as the *other Jane*. She hadn't quite thought about her appearing foreign from another Jane's perspective. She'd make a mental note of the concept.

"Yes. I'm the other Jane." Our Jane put out her hand and Jane Four seemed to think this was kind of funny, perhaps quaint. She shook it weekly with cold, clammy hands.

"So, what do we do?" Jane Four asked with a shrug.

"I thought we could walk by the pond. I'd like to ask a few questions. You know, just chat really, while I take notes."

"You came all the way from California to chat? That's very interesting," Jane Four stared off, giving it serious thought.

"I've got some standard questions, but I think I'm going to mix it up a little. Do you know which way we go to the pond?"

Jane Four looked around. "This way."

They left the visitor center, immediately immersed in nature. The path was clearly marked, railings to the side. It led through stunning pastoral scenes of every kind of green. Our Jane hiked in her part of Central California from time to time. The only green season was just after the skimpy rain, and for a month or so everywhere was green, then back to monotonous brown.

This was different. She felt the weight of time, of nature. The sky was only a pale blue, so the pond and the trees took the stage. It was peaceful, quiet, surrounded by the verdant trees. Jane Four seemed to be experiencing the same feeling. They both stayed quiet for the first few minutes. Our Jane pulled out her notebook, almost reluctantly. "Sorry, I got distracted by all this beauty. It's nice to think we share a name with this beautiful place."

"Yeah. I remember some teasing when I was a kid. Bad puns, mostly." Jane Four laughed, much like a snort, "Kids can be assholes."

"That's for sure. Okay, some questions. What's your middle name?"

"Emma." Jane Four shot her the question back, "Yours?"

"Emma, as a matter of fact. Wow, that's so cool. You're the first Jane Emma I've met so far. Maybe we're alike in other ways." Our Jane looked at the younger Janes attire again. She was trying very hard not to judge, but even though her jacket was colorful, threadbare was the dominant feature. Her jeans also had holes in them that weren't made on purpose. Her Vans shoes were in surprisingly good shape. The rest was all vagabond. Jane couldn't quite define the incongruities. She wasn't sure how to ask her about it, either.

She stuck to the easy questions. "How many times have you been to Walden pond?"

"Never." Jane Four shrugged.

"Wait. Really?"

"Yeah. I'm from Holyoke." Jane four pointed non-committally, "That's southeast of here."

"Sorry, I tried to research the geography before I left from California but I'm still a little lost. Your state is a lot different than mine."

"I bet. Cali is huge on the map. We have all the old shit, though. Holyoke is just south of Amherst College, if that helps."

"Okay. I've heard of Amherst."

The trail led them around the pond in an ebb and flow, sometimes close to the water, then totally surrounded by trees. Now they were only feet from the pond. It was stunning; modest and epic at the same time. Jane understood why it inspired the writer's imagination. Glassy before noon, the water made for picture taking. Jane snapped a few shots, then asked Jane for a selfie. Jane Four stood like a rag doll, no smiles. Jane made a mental note. *I guess not everyone like pictures of themselves.* She warmed a little on the third selfie together.

Our Jane recalled a line of Thoreau. She thought she had known what it meant. Now that she stood in the same place, she fully understood it - "'*I went to the woods because I wished to live deliberately. I wanted to live deep and suck out all the marrow of life.*' Jane had to force herself back into the reality. She smiled at the other Jane, "Have you read Henry Thoreau?"

"Not really. They made us read a little in high school. Holyoke Community hasn't pushed any more Thoreau at us yet."

"Oh, what are you majoring in?" Jane scribbled.

Jane Four shrugged. It seemed to be a signature move. "Don't know. I started out wanting to go to culinary school. That fizzled. I'm kinda just getting the basic stuff out of the way right now. I don't know, maybe I'll go into writing. Always liked English class. Although, they made us read some pretty boring books. I don't know why they made us read *The Bell Jar*. I wanted to literally kill myself after reading that book, ironically."

"Oh, my God! Sylvia Plath? I love that book," Our Jane admitted. "It is really sad, though."

"Yeah. *Too* sad. Who wants to read about electroshock therapy and insulin injections? Sylvia Plath is from Massachusetts. It's required reading in like every school in the state. Well written, sure, but yuck."

Our Jane laughed. "Okay, we'll have to disagree about that. Funny. I assumed you'd been to the pond since your last name is Walden. I guess I'm full of silly assumptions. I thought everyone loved the *Bell Jar*."

They both stared at the pond. Our Jane felt her questions were inadequate for this Jane. Maybe because their ages were close, she just wanted to talk with her. "It's beautiful here. Not sure I would live here in a cabin in the woods like Thoreau, but it is peaceful."

"Na. Me neither. I need, like, coffee and bars, and civilization, ya know? Anyway, so how does this work? I mean, are you going to take what I say down exactly and put in the book, or is this just like one scene in the book?"

"Scene? That's an interesting concept. Makes it sound like a play, or movie screenplay. Honestly, the other Janes I've met are older than me and I asked them some age-appropriate questions. But I truly don't know how the book is going to turn out." Our Jane felt an odd kinship, like she could really talk to this Jane. She let out a breath. "Cards on the table? I don't know what the hell I'm doing."

Jane Four stared at Our Jane, like she clicked into full engagement. "Now, that's interesting. Real honesty. I like that."

Our Jane took a deep breath of crisp New England air. "Wow, I feel like I've been holding my breath until I said that. I discussed it with Christian but..."

"Whose Christian? Like Christian Grey, from those hot books?"

Our Jane laughed. "Oh my God. He hates that the character is named Christian. He's my best friend. Christian agreed to come on this trip with me because he's helping his dad with his business."

Jane Four sported a quizzical look.

"He's selling California beer." Our Jane clarified. "Tring to open up markets for his dad's micro-brews."

"Wicked!"

"Ha! You actually said it. I have to be honest – I was waiting for you to say that particular word since I met you."

"I hate being a stereotype, but I love that frickin' word. Every time I say wicked I start cussing right after. It's like my gateway drug for swearing. I still live with Ma, so I try not to use it so much. My filter... well, it's kinda fucking broken."

Our Jane laughed. "Good. I need to mix shit up, to see what I'm doing. Because I'm not quite sure what this book is going to be. So I think I'll ask you a lot of random questions. Is that okay?"

"Shoot."

"Have a boyfriend?"

"I tend to have girlfriends. Had a few boyfriends in high school. I fall for the person, ya know? But I definitely gravitate towards girls."

"Oh. Cool. I didn't think of that." Our Jane tried to remember the particulars. "Wait, weren't there some hot guys on your Facebook page?"

"Yeah. Because abs. And I like guy backs as much as I like girl backs. Fuck if I know why. That's not a problem, is it?"

"Oh no. I don't care if you're gay, or bi, or whatever." Jane realized. "I just never occurred to me that one of the Jane Waldens would be."

Jane Four took an elaborate bow, and announced, "Definitely bi. Nice to meet ya.'"

"I've always kinda understood why a girl could be with another girl. I mean the female body is beautiful." Our Jane said with true candor. Then she sighed, "But I'm with you about abs. And guy's arms. I don't know if I could give those up."

"You should try it sometime. Not that I'm coming on to you, or anything."

"Oh no! I didn't think you were." Our Jane felt more relaxed than she'd been since the trip began. "Let's switch gears. Where do you work?"

"I'm in community college right now, not much time. Odd jobs, mostly."

"Odd jobs like convenience store, laundromat, retail? Or odd jobs like 'I could tell you, but I'd have to kill you' kind of jobs?"

Jane Four smiled and stared off, "Maybe I should keep it a mystery."

Our Jane marked the coy smirk of her lips, with her glossy sheen of lip balm. She reminded herself to describe it later just like that. She made some notes to try to capture the moment, the way she moved. It was almost hypnotic. Our Jane mused that Jane Four could probably get any sexual partner she wanted. There was an allure she could not put her finger on.

Jane Four tried to see what she was writing. "Okay. Now I feel like a lab rat. What did you write down about me?" She came dangerously close to Our Jane, trying to see. It wasn't threatening, but Jane hadn't had any close female friends for a while, and she pulled back, by an indefinable instinct.

Jane Four backed off with a dramatic arm gesture. "Whoa, jittery! Ha, Jittery Jane. I think that's what I'll call you." She turned to the pond, "What are we supposed to get from Walden Pond? What's the idea? Is this just a kind of stunt, or some giant analogy?"

"Hey, the kid catches on quick." Jane finished her notes.

"Kid? Hey now, we're like the same age, right?"

"About a year apart, unless you lied on your social media." Our Jane swung back toward the water. "Answer is, I don't know. I think the pond started as a gimmick. Now... now if feels like an analogy. So, I guess it's both. Now that I'm here, I'm worried about seeming pretentious."

They both inched closer to the shore. It just sat there, this beautiful, oddly shaped body of water. It had meant so much to Our Jane in ninth grade, when she'd discovered Thoreau – thanks to her favorite English teacher. She glanced down to see just the upper part of herself and Jane reflected into the water. Their images shimmied ever so slightly. Even though they were different heights, they could have been the same person, interchangeable Janes. But, wasn't that the point? Jane Waldens, both reflecting in Walden Pond. Suddenly, the analogy seemed silly, overly obvious.

Our Jane started to feel the pit of her stomach churn. Maybe it was the shimmering images, just out of focus and wavy enough to affect her belly.

"You okay, Jittery Jane?"

She proved her new nickname by starting at the other Jane's voice. "Sorry, I was just thinking that maybe this Walden Pond thing is too..."

"Over the top?" Jane Four smiled.

"Yes. That's it. I seem to be a little unfocused today. This book... well, a lot is riding on it. I keep realizing how much."

"Let's walk, Jittery Jane. Maybe that will help."

Jane Four took her arm in arm to get her to move. This time she didn't jump, appreciating the gesture. They walked linked, as though down the yellow brick road, without the dancing and singing, of course. The idea came into her mind that this other Jane, almost another physical part of her ego was helping her through her confusion while at Walden Pond. *Talk about pretentious analogies*, she thought.

They walked on a thin stretch of the beach. *Do you call it a beach next to a pond? Bank of the pond?* More confusing details she didn't know. Her confidence was paper thin. Our Jane brought herself back into focus. "Okay. Umm. How about family?"

"Oh." They unlinked, the intimacy broken. Jane Four reported, "Two brothers, a mom and dad. I'm the youngest. Not very exciting."

Jane made a note. "What do you do for fun?"

"Party, hang out, have sex, of course." Jane Four looked over with a grin. "How much honesty do you want?"

Our Jane smiled. "Total."

"I like to drink. I've never taken a drug I had to inject. Now that pot's legal in Mass, I partake, shall we say."

"You didn't before?"

"Of course, but now I openly admit it." Jane Four turned the tables, "You?"

"It's legal in Cali too, but not much. I've tried it. All I did was eat a Twinkie, then fell asleep."

"Umm. Is Twinkie a euphemism… an anagram… shit, are you trying to say you wanted a dick?"

Jane laughed louder than she thought Walden Pond deserved. *What would Thoreau think?* She caught herself. "No, actual Twinkies; the little processed cakes. I think I gained four pounds that night. You are definitely the bluntest Jane yet."

"It's weird thinking there are so many out there." Jane casually ran her fingers through her blue streaked hair.

"It is." Our Jane glanced at her counterpart, "And so different. But, the same too."

"Is that what the book is about?"

"I wish I knew what the book is about."

"I think you need to mix it up. Get out of your own head," Jane Four began removing her top. "Time for something crazy."

Our Jane froze. "What are you doing?"

Jane Four thought it was obvious. "Swimming. I saw the sign in the visitor's place, swimming's allowed."

"Do you have a suit?"

"Nope." She removed her clothes quickly and Jane was facing the backside of a very naked Jane, tattoos and all. Swiveling her head quickly to either side, Our Jane saw no one else around their general area. When she looked back to Jane Four, she was already in the water.

"Jane!" she whisper-shouted, feeling ridiculous. "I don't think you're supposed to do *that*."

"You think Henry David Thoreau swam in a speedo? Come on in. It's cold as fuck, but it will make a good chapter. Let's Thoreau this bitch."

*Thoroughly Thoureau-ed?* Our Jane thought.

Jane Four splashed. "Stop thinking and jump in."

"Not so loud," Our Jane looked around again. "I'll... I'll just watch you swim."

"That would make you a perv. Or a lesbian." Jane Four perked up at this. She over-exaggerated every word provocatively. "You sure you're not a lesbian? I think you could be." She rose herself out of the water, revealing the curve of her breasts, stopping before she revealed too much.

Our Jane rubbed her temples, sure the ruckus had caught attention. She scanned around, reasoning that random people could be exploring the surrounding woods, not focusing on swimmers. Jane knew she could never skinny dip. Maybe with Todd. But not with a stranger, in full daylight at a tourist attraction.

To her surprise, she felt her own hands fumble for her blouse. *Crazy Jane. I'm calling her Crazy Jane.* As if on cue, Crazy Jane did a cat call as Our Jane undressed. It should have mortified her, put for some reason it spurred her on. Her last practical thought was that she was glad she had recently shaved her legs. She took the plunge.

Our Jane had no idea how deep the pond was. She dunked under. She came back up quickly, right next to Jane. "Holy Shit, that's cold!"

Jane Four laughed. "Yep. *Wicked* cold. let's swim out and get warm. Move those muscles, girl."

Jane didn't want to move. She was already shivering, but Crazy Jane moved, so Our Jane followed. *I am literally swimming in my idea.* She realized this moment had to happen. She couldn't mention a body of water, then not take the plunge. It was more than the name Walden. Suddenly the metaphor didn't seem so silly; all thanks to Crazy Jane.

They swam out a little farther. She spun to look for Crazy Jane and found her staring, smiling, alluring.

"Is this enough for your wicked book?"

"Yeah." Our Jane scanned for others. "Yeah, I think we better get back to shore."

Crazy Jane continued her stare. Jane had never consciously gotten attention from a female before. She had several lesbian friends, but they were all coupled, no interest in her. Before she could be sure Jane was even giving those signals, she was swimming back to shore. Our Jane followed.

Before they even reached the shore, Our Jane saw the park ranger standing by their clothes. *Where did he come from?* Crazy Jane had reached the shore first.

The ranger spoke to Crazy Jane. "Ma'am, we don't allow nude…"

Jane either wasn't listening, or didn't care. Walking out of the water, she wasn't shy. The ranger clumsily turned his back from the nudity. He was around 30, slender, not tall. Jane nonchalantly began dressing. Jane noticed the tattoos on her upper legs were orange and red flames. There hadn't been any tattoos on her back, and realized with a blush that she'd assumed someone as wild as Jane would have a back tatt. *Am I really that judgmental?*

Our Jane covered herself as she emerged from the water. "I'm so sorry, officer."

"Ranger, ma'am."

"Ranger, sorry." She dressed. "It was just an impulse. I guess the beauty of the pond, you know…"

Crazy Jane gesticulated toward the ranger. "We don't have to explain anything to this pig."

"Ma'am. I'd appreciate it if you didn't..."

"Jane! Sorry, Mr. ranger. We were just so overcome with this place." Our Jane shot a glance to Crazy Jane. Crazy was not backing down.

"Are you done? Can we go?" Crazy Jane said, only inches from the man's face. "Gonna give us a ticket, cop?"

"Ma'am, I'm not a cop, or a pig. I'm not even a policeman. If you promise to..."

"We're not making any promises, ranger man. This is the people's park, you fascist. You think old Henry didn't skinny dip? Shit, he probably pissed in this pond all the time."

The Ranger had had enough. "Okay, ladies, time to leave."

"How dare you!" Crazy Jane lived up to her new moniker. "I pay my taxes, you skinny little shit!"

The park ranger ushered them out, around the visitor's center, and toward the front of the park entrance. All the while, witnesses in the form of families, grandparents, and decent folk of all sorts listened to Crazy Jane dress down the poor ranger. The word fascist was repeated several times, along with 'dirty screw,' 'small-penis' and 'Walden Warden.' Our Jane was mortified, but did smile to herself at Crazy Jane's energy.

They were promptly thrown out of the park. Our Jane was impressed with the reserve the ranger showed, despite the verbal ravages of Crazy Jane. No other authorities got called, they were just made to leave. The two Janes walked the long trail on the edge of Route 126 that skirted the park. No one told them how far from the park they had to stay, so they continued until they reached the intersection of Highway 2. Jane called Christian, and he agreed to meet them there.

"I can't believe we did that." said Our Jane, who'd finally stopped shivering after the long trek out of the park.

Crazy Jane said, "One more thing off my bucket list. Get thrown out of a state park."

"Next stop, Yellowstone," Our Jane offered.

Crazy Jane laughed. "That's the one with the geysers, right? Yeah, they couldn't keep me behind any barriers. I want to see that shit up close."

"You might make our name famous before I do. 'Jane Walden, serial park crasher goes on wild spree.'"

"I like it," Crazy Jane said excitedly, "Hey, I could do it as publicity for the book." Jane got serious. "By the way, how much are you paying for my story?"

Jane nearly choked. "Umm... I don't... I mean, there's no..."

Crazy Jane smiled wide. "Ha, ha! I'm just kidding. It'll be fun being in a book. Will you send me a copy, at least?"

"Oh course! If I can actually get to the finish line and get this thing published, you'll get one of the first seven copies. Promise."

"Cool. So, what happens now?"

"What do you mean?" Jane looked around at their predicament.

"Well," said Crazy Jane with her signature shrug. "if the official interview is over, can you hang out for a while?"

"Oh. I don't know." Our Jane furrowed her brow. "I'll have to check with Christian. He's the schedule keeper."

"Ahh, him again. Is Christian hot, or what?"

"Christian? No!" Our Jane heard her own words. "Okay, that sounded mean. He's cute. He's kinda thin."

"Nice ass?"

"Hey, he's my best friend. I don't look at his ass."

"Liar."

"Okay," our Jane laughed, "flat as this highway. No ass at all. His arms and chest are okay. Wait, you're into girls."

"I told you I'm bi. Besides, that slutty author made the name Christian hot."

Our Jane reminisced. She read the "Grey" trilogy just like all of her friends. "They were so badly written though."

Crazy Jane shrugged, "She's still rich and famous."

"True."

"Anyway, if you can't hang out now, I know of a few parties lined up tonight. Wanna come?"

"Hmm. I don't know. I'll see what Christian thinks."

"Sound like you're a couple to me."

"Oh, stop! When you meet Christian, you'll know we are just friends."

"Oh shit, I just remembered my ride flaked on me. Could you take me into Boston? It's not that far."

"I'm sure we can do that." Just then, Christian pulled up. "Oh, and here's our ride."

He carefully pulled to the side of the busy highway, and the girls jumped in. A few cars honked at him.

Our Jane said, "Hey buddy. Jane needs a ride into Boston. Okay if we take her?"

Crazy Jane wasted no time. "Hi Christian. Jane said you were cute. I think those glasses make you hot."

"Hi back." Christian adjusted said glasses. "You're pretty cute yourself. What else did she say about me? And why are you both wet?"

Crazy Jane said, "She said you have a flat ass."

Christian shrugged. "She's right. Total pancake country back there." He turned to our Jane, "Please stop checking out my ass, it's getting embarrassing."

"Oh, shut up." Our Jane said. "She *asked* about your ass."

"That's right. I did. I was trying to figure out if you were hot like that character in *50 Shades*."

"Oh God, I hate those books – for ruining my name, if nothing else."

Crazy Jane leaned up to the front seat. "Well, you're definitely on the hot meter."

"Thanks. Coming at me pretty hard there, Massachusetts Jane."

Our Jane chimed in, "You may be safe; she's into girls right now."

"I said I'm flexible," she eyed Christian again. "Hey, so I invited you and Jane to some parties tonight. Can you and your *girlfriend* make it tonight?"

"Janes not my girlfriend," Christian declared. "What time?"

"Wait, you'd want to go?" Jane's assumptions were shattering all around her. "I thought you'd be worried about getting to New York."

"We have a cushion of time. We can stay over tonight, then leave in the morning. It's just over four hours from Boston to New York City. I think we can indulge."

Our Jane didn't hide her surprise, "Well, that was easy."

Christian looked in the rear-view mirror as he drove, "So, Back Seat Jane – can we crash overnight at one of these parties?"

Our Jane wasn't sure this was her Christian. "You feeling okay? Did something happen? Did you sell a lot of beer?"

"Nope. Not one damn case. Total failure. Ask me why I'm okay with partying tonight," Christian said.

From the back seat, crazy Jane blurted, "Why?"

"Cause I'm it a 'screw it' mood. Time to drink and party. Massachusetts has some crazy alcohol rules, which complicated things. Should have seen this coming - four stops, no sales, so I say screw it!"

Our Jane patted his arm. "Sorry Christian. You really made four sales stops while Jane and I were swimming?"

"Aha. Swimming, were you? That explains it." he cocked an eyebrow.

"I'll fill you in later."

"I can't wait for that story. Yes, Four stops, zero sales."

Crazy Jane asked, "Haven't saved Dad's business yet, huh?"

Christian looked to Our Jane, "She knows a lot. You bonded?" He looked in the rear view. "Nope, haven't saved anyone yet. Maybe I'll make some money back in New York…"

"Money back?" Jane said, confused.

"Sorry, it's complicated. We'll talk about it later, after the swimming story." he said, hoping she would forget.

"We also got thrown out of the park." Crazy Jane offered.

Christian said, "Okay. I want the story now."

Crazy Jane changed the subject, "Sounds like it's a night to celebrate, party, and forget."

"Yes. Yes, it is." Christian smiled into the rear-view mirror.

Our Jane felt a pang she didn't expect. She knew it couldn't be jealousy, but was surprised by how close it felt to that very thing.

# Chapter 9

# Tourists

"Experience is never wasted." – Joanna Penn

Growing up in California, Jane had been to lots of different cities of all sizes. As a family, they had travelled extensively. However, she'd never been to any large East Coast cities. The feel was much different than western urban centers. Boston was an old city that had modernized over time, but she wasn't ready for the roundabouts. If you've ever experienced a roundabout with one or two lanes, it will not prepare you for a 5-lane roundabout in a very busy, often impatient city like Boston. Even in the passenger seat, they are harrowing.

Fate worried for Christian as he white knuckled through the first busy roundabout, and felt terrible when he got off in the wrong lane. She gently told him she was recalculating, and soon got him back on track. The GPS knew she would be announcing more roundabouts shortly. She made note of the other, new Jane in the back seat, who smiled wickedly. Oh dear, here we go, thought Fate.

Crazy Jane was helpful from the back seat. As Our Jane and Christian soon found out, Bostonians were fond of honking, especially if they smelled weakness, or tourists, or both. Crazy Jane happily flipped off all honkers. Flashing her middle finger with practiced ease, she invited a few extra honks with her actions. She smiled and laughed, seeming to be on an adventure in the wild streets.

They were told it was okay to double park to let Crazy Jane out. She handed Our Jane a scribbled address and told them to meet up around seven. She jumped out, flipping off the honker, who was trying to communicate that double parking was indeed *not okay.*

After Crazy Jane was out and away, Christian asked, "That leaves several hours to bum around Boston. Want to be tourists?"

"Yes! We've been in such a hurry, it's about time we slowed down. Oh. My. God. Is that the *Cheers* bar? We have to go!" exclaimed Our Jane.

Christian laughed, remembering the summer they had done little else except watch 1980's sitcoms. They got through *The Bill Cosby Show, Full House, Different Strokes,* and *Cheers* before their senior high school year started.

"Let me find a place to park." The dutiful Christian announced.

They parked at a paid garage and walked the 1/3 of a mile to the *Cheers* bar. They passed the Boston Commons (The Massachusetts version of Central Park). Using Jane's phone, they plotted some other touristy things they could do after hitting the bar.

Like in the show, Cheers was located downward from street level. The biggest difference from the show, and the actual bar, was the gift shop area selling all things *Cheers!* Cardboard cut-outs of the cast from the show, beer mugs, trinkets of every kind. The place was packed.

They finally got a bar table and ordered the themed "Norm Burger" for Christian, and "Carla's Pasta" dish for Jane. She relayed her day with Crazy Jane. Christian nearly choked on his burger when she got to the part about skinny dipping, and the Ranger harangue.

Christian said, "I wish you'd told me before I agreed to party with her tonight."

"You did agree pretty quickly." Jane wasn't sure she wanted to know the answer, "Are you hot for Jane Walden?"

"I see what you did there. I'm ignoring the double meaning. She's intriguing, nothing more. She's going to be a great chapter of the book. Maybe two."

"She is. I wonder what will happen tonight?" She gave him one last chance. "We can back out if you want."

Christian dunked some fries in ketchup. "She'd probably track us down. No, let's cut loose tonight. We've earned it."

"*Cheers* to that." they raised their glasses, both groaning at the bad pun. They drank to it anyway.

After lunch, they strolled through Boston Commons. Jane looked on her phone for information, and spoke it aloud as though she were a tour guide, "Established in 1634, Boston Common is America's oldest park. Ooooh, it says public shaming used to happen here. You might have found someone in stocks here, or oh my... people hanging from the Great Elm. That turned dark quickly. Oh good, the tree isn't here anymore."

"Why? Do you see dead people?" Christian mused. "I bet there are a lot of ghosts here."

Jane socked Christian in the arm. "Stop it. You know I believe in that shit."

Christian changed to a whisper, "Here Jane. I died right here. Help me Jane..."

Jane landed a solid blow on Christian's arm again.

"Still doesn't hurt."

Jane went back to her phone. "I'll hurt you one day."

"I have no doubt," answered Christian. Jane thought she noticed an odd tone, but dismissed it as Christian asked, "What other touristy things are in walking distance?"

She consulted her all-powerful phone. "Boston University is just over there, MIT is across the Charles River. That's the Charles River, by the way. Fenway Garden Society, The Boston Library, Boston Opera House. Boston Duck Tours? Duck Tours? Wait. What is this nonsense?"

She clicked on her screen and was met with a picture of a very peculiar looking vehicle. "Interesting. It gives you a tour on land, then in the water. That's cool!"

"Really?" Christian tried to get the concept. "Like touring Boston in a transformer?"

"Kinda." Jane analyzed the metaphor, "Not really, it can only go on land or water. No battling robots. Wait, here's a video of one going into the water."

Christian watched the short video and nodded. "Okay. That is pretty cool. Duck boat, my lady?"

"Duck Boat," she took Christian's arm, "for sure."

It was a brisk walk to the Duck Tours area, but they were not disappointed. Their vehicle was light blue, with three sets of tires. The front resembled the curved bow of a ship. There was even a prop anchor near the driver's side door. The vehicle was covered, almost like a wheel house on a boat deck, and had a cartoon duck painted on the side.

It was driven by a self-proclaimed conDUCK-tor, who talked them through sites like the State House, Bunker Hill, Copley Square, and even talked about the big dig, a controversial ten-year project that re-vamped and enlarged Boston's driving mess. Which everyone admitted was still a mess. Then they headed right into the Charles River.

The conDUCKtor assured them that their converted WWII style amphibious vehicle was perfectly safe. It was an odd moment driving into the water. But soon they were on a boat, not a car, powering along the Charles River.

Their guide, full of bad puns and jokes, made it a touristy delight. Christian was dubious of the claim that Boston was the "birthplace of Freedom," but he and Jane were fascinated by some new factoids. Jane's favorite was about where the Boston Tea Party happened, it being no longer a harbor, or water at all; It was filled in years ago and now is on solid land. "No dumping tea in Boston harbor, unfortunately." She said aloud.

"I guess not." Christian lamented.

"This guide is good," Jane said, and squawked like a duck. Not knowing where that came from, she covered her mouth and laughed.

Christian laughed back, "You just like all the puns."

"Guilty."

Christian shook his head. "How can you be a writer and love terrible puns?"

"I love words, I love being clever. Sometimes, I like a good fart joke." Jane turned away dramatically. "I'm very complicated."

"That's for sure. But I think I've figured you out."

"If you don't know me by now, Mister Christian, I fear you never will."

"Oh no, I got you," said Christian, "I just hope you have yourself figured out."

"Meaning what?"

"I mean the Jane I know wouldn't just jump into a pond naked with a stranger."

"There's nothing wrong with being impulsive sometimes."

"Not at all." Christian agreed. "But, did you do it out of impulse, because Jane did it, or because it would be good for the book?"

Jane answered quickly, "All of the above."

"Good. You're getting closer."

"Closer to what?" sometimes Christian's vagueness did not charm her. "Why are you talking in riddles?"

"I'm not. My secret thesis is that you are not entirely self-aware. Well, not enough. Let's say unexamined. I liked this *Seven Ways to Jane* idea so much, because it means you are digging into who you are, what you want."

"I don't think any of us are truly self-aware. I know what I want. Don't I already have a handle on that?" *Definitely un-charming, Christian.* "Why are you planting these time bombs of self-doubt in my head?"

"I'd never do that. Just the opposite. I think a good writer has to see people, situations, see 'the wires' just behind the circuit board of human interaction, especially in themselves."

"That's a big, pretentious sentence there," Jane warned, "be careful you don't fall in."

Christian ignored that and continued. "Bottom line, I think this is a great experience for you. It will lead to good things."

The conversation was getting strange. Jane steered it elsewhere. "Dear Christian, my buddy, my pal, let's just have fun tonight. 'Just screw it,' remember? How long until we meet Crazy Jane?"

"90 minutes. I like that moniker – Crazy Jane. Does she know you call her that?"

Jane shrugged, "She'll find out when the book comes out. If the book…"

"When," Christian admonished. "You were right the first time. No self-doubt allowed."

"Okay, okay, *when* the book comes out. Who knows, maybe I'll have another nickname for you after tonight."

It was beginning to get dark, the fun day promising to yield to an even better night. Jane reminded herself to confirm the "surprise" for Christian. A tug of doubt returned, dancing around her resolve. She put it away. *It's all about Christian, for once.* She phoned from the bathroom - all confirmed. Now, to experience a night with Crazy Jane.

# Chapter 10

# Screw It

"Anyone can hold the helm when the sea is calm." –
Cyrus

They met Jane at the address, a famous Boston Tavern called the Green Dragon. They'd walked, leaving the car safely in the parking garage. Who knew how the night might go? Besides fate, of course. No point paying multiple times to park all over Boston, they had agreed.

The Green Dragon was smaller than they expected, packed with people. They found Crazy Jane in the back of the tavern, taking a shot. A half full beer glass in her other hand. She was sitting with a man about their age, maybe a little older. He was bearded, and had a scraggly appearance; torn jeans which did not just look factory aged, glasses, and a genuinely dirty ball cap. Instead of the big Red 'B' to signify the Boston Red Socks, it had a picture of two red cartoon socks. He reluctantly looked up from his phone as they arrived.

"Oh, hey," Crazy Jane said with no enthusiasm. "Welcome to the famous Green Dragon, the most boring, overrated tavern in Boston."

"Are you kidding?" Christian beamed as he looked around, "This is the place where the Sons of Liberty met. The Boston tea party was planned right here. Paul Revere was sent from this tavern on his ride."

The two native Massachusans looked at him blankly. Jane's friend spoke up, "Yeah, we learned that when we were like five. Boston is boring."

"This is my friend Jesse." Crazy Jane pointed to Mr. Scraggly. "He hates everything, except me."

Our Jane said, "I'm not sure how to respond to that, but okay."

Christian went to shake Jesse's hand, who reluctantly returned it with a weak shake before disengaging.

Jesse was not giving off a party vibe. The bar table they'd gotten only had two chairs, so they stood awkwardly close by. There were vignettes of people everywhere, pressing in on them. It was very warm. Our Jane broke the awkwardness, "I guess we'll go get a drink. Is it Happy Hour?"

Christian's left brain kicked in, "No happy hours or bar specials in Massachusetts. It's against state law. Also, there is a 2-drink limit here, pitchers for 2 or more people only, and eight towns in the state are still totally dry."

Jesse scowled. Crazy Jane looked confused, "Why the fuck do you know all that?"

Christian shrugged. "Research for my job."

"Well, it proves my point. Boston equals boring. Let's go somewhere else," suggested Crazy Jane.

"Like where?" asked Christian.

Our Jane lit up. "Hey, is Salem around here? Maybe we could go there?"

"Salem? It's so touristy." Jesse scoffed. "Plus, it's like 45 minutes away."

Both Jane and Christian were disappointed, but Christian shrugged. "Okay, what do you suggest?"

"Ever been to Provincetown?" Crazy Jane smiled.

"First time to Massachusetts, remember? Our Jane reminded, then added with a smile, "No ponds to swim in there, I hope?"

"Just the ocean, if you really want to swim. P-town is at the tip of the cape."

"How far is it from here?" asked Christian.

"Not far by ferry." She sweetened the pot for Christian, "Lots of history stuff there."

Jesse stared at Christian. "Not afraid of a few queer folks, are you?"

"Got no problem with anyone, as long as they don't have a problem with me." Christian smiled.

Our Jane asked, "Fun place?"

"Super fun," confirmed Crazy Jane. "I have a friend whose dad owns a house there. They're rich, one per-centers, but the daughter's still cool. We could see P-town, then hit the party at her house."

"Sounds fun," said Christian, before our Jane could answer.

Jesse seemed to have a whole set of assumptions about Christian. *Why the instant resentment?* thought Jane. She wondered if Christian would play the party animal, just to wipe the smug judgment off Jesse's face. *Christian, who are you right now?*

Jesse shrugged at the decision. Jane couldn't make Jesse out beyond his surly manner. She wasn't sure anything could make him happy, but he seemed relieved to be away from the Green Dragon. They walked out onto the sidewalk.

Crazy Jane stared at her watch, the face on the inside of her wrist. "Oh, shit. we'd better hurry."

"Why?" asked Christian.

"So, we can have a wicked good time!" yelled Crazy Jane.

They hurried down the street. Turned out the dock with the ferry wasn't far. Crazy Jane and Jesse took out tickets they already had. Crazy Jane whispered into Our Janes ear, "They're fake season passes. Shhh. Sorry, we only have two."

They got to the ticket box, where they saw the rates. "It's how much?" asked Christian of the ticket person. He tried not to show his shock, and shelled out the nearly $90 per person, round trip tickets. Jane was getting more and more concerned about money. She felt a blush at realizing the details of funding the trip had all been left to poor Christian, with his dad's money. She would find a way to make it up to him. *Maybe his surprise could be a down payment,* she thought.

Their ferry was a two-layered affair, with blue seats along the top. Part open area, part closed off section with large windows all around. They opted for the open area. Our Jane was disappointed that the chairs all faced the same way, toward the front. Fearing that conversation might be stifled, Crazy Jane and Jesse sat in front of them. She seemed comfortable swiveling around in her own chair to engage. Crazy Jane promised, "You're going to love P-town, even you Christian."

Christian shot a quizzical *what-have-you-told-her-about-me?* look at Our Jane, but didn't say anything.

Our Jane ignored the look and read the brochure, "It says it take 90 minutes. That's twice the time it would've taken to Salem."

"Yes, but Salem is booooooring." Crazy Jane elaborated, "Pretend witches, shops with power crystals." She looked at Jane with a wink, "Though I hear, they dance naked in the woods, sometimes." Then the devilish look vanished, "Unfortunately, I've seen a lot of these 'Wiccans.' Most are fat, middle-aged lesbians. Why do the ugliest people always want to take off their clothes? It's the same with nudists."

Even Jesse laughed at that.

Crazy Jane put her arm around Jesse. "You'll have to forgive my buddy, here. He just broke up with his boyfriend."

"He wasn't my *boyfriend*," he said with disdain at the term, "I'm not in Junior High."

"Sorry," Crazy Jane rolled her eyes, like she was still in Junior High. "Your partner, your lover."

Jesse shook his head, "Shut up Jane, we're in the same boat."

"Yep, I was dumped too." Jane dramatically played with her blue-streaked hair. "And the best cure for us bitches is hedonism. Maybe a little debauchery thrown in. If you play your cards right, maybe P-town will convert you both. Your guides are both dedicated homosexuals out for a good time."

"I thought you were bi?" Our Jane cocked a friendly brow. "More secrets, other Jane?"

"Secrets is a strong word," Crazy Jane cocked her head, "I don't think that way. I just follow what feels right to me." She put her arms in the air, letting the wind blow through her hands.

Our Jane wondered if it was too easy an analogy to say that Crazy Jane goes where the wind blows her. She dug for her notebook, but slid it back into her bag. She decided tonight was a night for experience. She could make notes tomorrow. *I'm going to watch Crazy Jane very closely tonight.*

During lags in conversation on the 90-minute trip, Jane and Christian had both been googling Province-town on their phones. They were now abreast of the history, but not ready for the site of the actual place. They arrived after dark. Disembarking, even at night, they were immediately charmed by the town.

Though P-town, as locals affectionately knew it, was the location where the 1620 pilgrims actually touched land first, they would sail to the mainland later to settle. The landscape was dominated by a Pilgrim monument, a tower that rose over 250 feet. But it was the 18th and 19th century that had written the firmest history upon this stretch of land. The whaling trade had put a permanent aesthetic on the place, with neat rows of ex-ship captain houses, of varying degree of grandeur and repair. There was a flurry of boats in the harbor, and the main streets were narrow and lined with people of all ages. This place seemed built for night life: Neon light, strings of Christmas-style lights, and shop windows all lit up the night with excitement.

Both our heroes noticed gay couples right away. No shy folks walked the streets of Provincetown, and both Jane and Christian thought of San Francisco as a parallel. Jane also thought of New Orleans. It wasn't the architecture that inspired this impression, but the people meandering through narrow streets, festooned with bright primary colors. Streamers and banners were erected across the streets, promoting festivals and upcoming events.

There were lots of playhouses and cabarets interwoven with gift shops and restaurants. The unmistakable aroma of clam chowder and seafood was everywhere, also a reminder of San Francisco. A plethora of rainbow flags and windsocks flew freely.

"Too much gay for you, *Christian*?" Jesse asked.

"Is that what it is, my *name* that makes you assume I'm uptight? Dude, my parents just liked the name. That's all." Christian looked around. "I think this is all great. It seems so free, laid back. It's kind of awesome.

I got no problem with anyone, dude. You're judging the wrong prude."

Our Jane added, "Remember guys, we're from California. We're open to anything. Besides, Christian is Jewish, ironically."

"Jane…" Christian began.

Crazy Jane interrupted, "Up for anything, you say?" Our Jane wasn't sure if she was flirting with Christian, or her. Crazy Jane's universal sexiness was shining bright.

Jesse's default animosity took a break, "Whatever. Let's hit a cabaret or drag show, then we'll go to Purgatory."

Christian smiled, pushed up his glasses. "I'm guessing that's not a metaphor?"

"No. It's a club." Jesse actually smiled. "All that P-Town has to offer."

"You sure you're up for this?" Our Jane whispered to Christian.

"Absolutely. Besides, the last ferry is leaving soon."

"Really?" Jane looked back to the ferry area.

"Yep. I think that's why they hurried us here." Christian smiled, arm around Jane's shoulder. "No turning back now."

They took in a drag show. There was a two-drink minimum, and to Christian's surprise, Jesse said he'd pay for the show, drinks, and food.

Christian took the good fortune, and the strain off the budget. Our Jane patted him on the knee at the news, and the good times prevailed. They had great food, most of the appetizers and dishes containing seafood. They were on Cape Cod, after all. The show was a review; some live music, some lip-synch. Mostly show tunes, and more than a few vaudeville style stand-up comedy bits between songs. Plenty of puns for Jane.

There were lots of political themed jokes, and Jane wondered at the mirror image quality of their left coast San Francisco, and this right coast P-town. She even wondered if folding the US in half like a map, if Provincetown and San Francisco would line up. Her geography knowledge still shaky, Jane dismissed the image, but the notion of a mirror image kept returning to her throughout the night: Jane and Christian, Jesse and Jane.

The drinks were heavy pours. "Whoa. That is a drink alright." Christian could feel the effect even before he got his second.

"Don't forget to pace, buddy boy," Our Jane warned, feeling the strangeness of a sudden role reversal. *Am I the responsible one tonight?*

"You're right…" Christian looked at them all. "Nope. No Designated Driver tonight. The last ferry left, we're here for the night. Screw it!"

The all raised their glasses, and agreed in unison, "Screw it!"

# Chapter 11

# Purgatory

"And yet to every bad there is a worse." – Thomas
Hardy

Purgatory turned out to be a basement club under a
place called Gifford House. The ceiling was low, and
as soon they walked in, there was a sea of flesh. A vast
number of shaved heads of all ages sat atop men that
were mostly shirtless. A great majority wore speedos
or a skimpy equivalent.

Our Jane remarked, "I thought you'd take us to a
lesbian bar."

"That was a lesbian cabaret we saw," Crazy Jane
reasoned. "Gotta mix up the gays."

Christian laughed. Jesse allowed a half smile. As
they descended, the music was too loud to hold a normal conversation. They waded through the under-
ground bodies, many giving Christian the nod of approval, or in some cases, possible interest. He thought

to himself how funny it was that the typical male to male nod across the room meant something totally different in a gay bar. He turned his attention to Jane, wondering how good her mental notes would be, a few drinks in.

Crazy Jane led Our Jane to the bar. Both Janes looked back to make sure the boys were following. Christian smiled widely, taking in the atmosphere. Jesse was last, scanning around for anyone interesting, Jane presumed. Jesse's face was still petulant, but she noticed his body gently kept the beat of the music, like a Pavlovian dance experiment.

Jane tried not to look at the sea of male torsos. Many of them were older, some hairy and some not, but there were good looking men woven throughout, mostly in very skimpy shorts. She forced herself to keep her eyes above the waists, mostly. She suddenly thought of Todd. *Such a jerk, such a good body. I bet Gabriel Oak would not be caught dead in a gay bar.* The thought made her giggle out loud.

Jane put eyes forward just in time, avoiding a sweaty man in front of her. She stopped in time, and was surprised to spot many women in the crowd.

"Why would lesbians come here?" Our Jane yelled in Crazy Jane's ear.

"Same reason I do, to support my gay and queer brethren." She turned toward the bartender, "Four shots of tequila and four beers please. Umm, just the house beer. Thanks."

Our Jane wanted to frame the question just right. "Why 'queer'? Why not just 'gay'? I've never quite got that."

"It's complicated. Jesse, like me, is always exploring gender stuff, sexuality. When he finally realized he only likes men, he wanted to be called queer. He wants to take back that word from assholes that use it to, I don't know, cause damage, I guess."

That got the attention of the older gentleman that Jane had almost bumped into. "Yeah, that's because the little shit didn't ever get beat up because he was a *queer.*"

The boys arrived to hear the end of the exchange. "What's going on?" Christian asked, trying to be heard over the crowd.

"Are you the *queer*?" the older man turned on Christian.

Christian stayed calm, despite the aggressive tone. "I'm just here for a drink, sir."

The old man poked Christian in the chest. "Don't 'sir' me. I used to play smear the queer for real. I was the queer. You kids have no idea what we went through to make the world safe for little fags like you."

Christian stood his ground. Jane thought it odd the older man would be offended by the word queer, but call Christian an even more offensive word. To Jane, it was equivalent to the N word. Maybe it was a word only the gay community could use without stigma or penalty.

A smaller man, about the same age (but with his shirt on), put his arm around the aggressive man. "Willy, honey, come on. Let these nice young people alone."

"I'm the queer." announced Jesse boldly. "And thanks, old man, for all you did, but the community is changing. We have to take back all those words they used to hurt us. You're lucky I don't go around calling myself a faggot!"

Jane and Christian shot each other a look, knowing trouble had arrived.

"Shit, Jesse," said Crazy Jane. Our Jane thought, *if Crazy Jane thinks that's too far...*

The old man Willy raised his fist, but his companion stopped him. That didn't matter, since the suddenly toxic words had been heard by others. The music was still going, but now the group of four was surrounded by angry men of all ages.

Behind her, Crazy Jane yelled, "Oww!" as a lesbian not over four feet tall pulled her hair. Crazy Jane yelled, "What's your stake in this, lady?"

Instead of answering, the short woman grabbed the freshly delivered beer. It splashed toward Crazy Jane's face like a sticky wave. Crazy Jane saw it coming, ducked in time, and the wrong Jane got drenched.

Pushing began from many directions, and Jesse was shouting fiercely at Willy, now barely restrained by his partner. Our Jane couldn't tell what he was shouting, as beer has splashed in one ear, and people shouted all around.

The pushing continued, but luckily it was toward the exit. Jane clutched to her wet bag, and Christian's arm. No punches were thrown, it was clear they were being pushed out, exiled. Crazy Jane managed to avenge her fellow Jane and got a random man in the face with a glass of beer. He seemed totally baffled, as he wasn't in the pushing group. Crazy Jane seemed to be enjoying herself. Jesse was facing the crowd, shouting defiant garbled nonsense, like a protestor being pushed out of his own debate.

When they made it to the stairs going up and out, the pushing stopped and they left the basement club behind.

Jesse paced back and forth. "Stupid old men think they own the movement!"

Crazy Jane pulled on one of Jesse's arm to get him to stop. "Shhh. It's over. Let's get to the real party."

As though he didn't hear her, he shouted back toward the club, "It's called LGBT – *Q* for a reason, assholes!" Some random couple made a wider circle around Jesse as they walked on.

Our Jane was looking for something to wipe her face. She found her last tissues in a plastic travel pack, and she and Christian each took one, both wiping her face.

When she looked up, Christian was smiling, "You okay?"

For an answer, his smile inspired one of her own, turning quickly into laughter. Soon Crazy Jane and Jesse were laughing too. Our Jane didn't think Jesse laughed very often, but the mood was lightening, a reset to the evening.

Christian said, "Well, we made it out of Purgatory. Metaphor complete. Is the real party going to be Heaven or Hell?"

"That's up to us. Ready for more adventure?" Crazy Jane looked to Christian. "I figured when the couple of drinks wore off, you'd want to …"

"To what? For non-judgmental LGBT- Q members, you've got me all wrong. I'm not a stuck-up prude." Instead of retorting Jesse's aggressiveness, Christian tried the opposite tack. He smiled, "If there's a party, let's go."

"Alright then," Jesse seemed to snap out of his moodiness, and reassessed Christian. "This way."

Crazy Jane laced her arm in our Jane's and off they marched. Our Jane's buzz was wearing off, and she had been pleasantly surprised, again, at Christian's determination to party. As they walked past rows of quaint houses that were surely 200 years old, some older, she looked at the narrow streets. Happy people were bunched in groups everywhere they looked, presumably bustling off to their own good times.

Mental notes were being taken, and Jane toyed with the metaphor of walking along the yellow brick road again. She didn't bother to cast the four of them into specific roles, as the metaphor would probably fall apart. She knew she wasn't in Kansas anymore, as cliché as that was. Glancing to Christian, she thought, *if he wants to party, he's earned it. I'll be his wing woman for tonight.* Jane laughed out loud at her mixing of anachronistic metaphors. Christian eyed her suspiciously, but smiled wryly, as though he had been invited to the internal metaphor party.

They were led to a fairly large, two-story house. Colonial was the only way to describe it to herself. Jesse saw Jane's interest. "Like it? It was built for a Captain and his wife around 1820. Built with Whaler money, big enough to support a large family."

"How many kids did he have?" asked Our Jane.

"None. Sadly, he was lost at sea." Jesse pointed to the roof, "His wife built that widow's watch up there on the roof, so she could see him come back. She died a widow here in the 1880's."

Crazy Jane took over the conversation. "My friend's parents are rich. She stays here rent free, while the parents live in their real house in Florida. First world problems, right?"

"What does your friend do?" Our Jane stared at the obviously expensive house.

"Rebecca's figuring it out. Floating after college, you know? Trying hard not to follow Daddy into international shipping."

Christian grasped the scenario. "So, she just parties all the time."

"Yep."

"Must be nice," Our Jane said.

They knocked at the door, answered within a minute. Like the Purgatory bar, the man was naked except for a black leather speedo, early twenties, wearing sunglasses. "Come in, *come* all. But not too fast – and always wear protection." The man laughed at his own dirty joke.

Jane was surprised that he had a California, classic surfer-dude accent. He was obviously wasted, and might've fallen over if not for the door handle he held onto. Christian and Jane exchanged a glance, standing directly behind Crazy Jane and Jesse. To Our Jane's surprise, it was Christian that shrugged with a "why not?" expression. They entered, either Heaven or Hell.

In the 1800's it must have seemed like a huge, vast house, but as Jane looked around the two-story home, she was surprised by how small it seemed inside. Especially since it was filled with people. There were dozens of people in various degrees of intoxication. People of all sexes were making out in corners. It reminded Jane of a no-parents high school party, rather than a millionaire's hang-out.

Crazy Jane tapped a man on a shoulder. Standing at the foot of the stairs, dressed in an expensive looking dark suit, he resembled plain-clothes security. He was also wearing sunglasses.

"Where's Rebecca?" probed Crazy Jane.

The man just pointed up the stairs. *Definitely not security.* They went up the stairs to the second floor, four doors met them. One was open and there were two bodies writhing together, still clothed. For the moment. Crazy Jane took a guess and headed up one more flight to what turned out to be the roof and widow's watch.

"Dirty Jane!" screamed a voice from the edge of the roof, as a red headed woman ran toward her.

"Rich-Bitch Becks!" screamed Jane as they collided. Being well over six feet tall, Rebecca lifted Jane off her feet with a swirling hug. They smacked a kiss on the lips and Jane was returned to the wood decking.

Crazy Jane touched her lips and said, "Don't start something unless you're going to finish. Holy shit! What is that?" Jane grabbed Rebecca's hand and stared at her ring finger.

"Like it? I found *the one*. Meet Michael." On cue, a man a little older than Rebecca walked into view. He was dressed in a business suit, no tie. He might have been a movie star, Our Jane thought, as he flashed a practiced smile. He shook Crazy Jane's hand first, then each of theirs in turn. Hellos were said all around. Jesse was last and seemed to disdain the human contact.

"No more epic trips to the sack, then?" Crazy Jane smiled, clearly a test of how much information Rebecca shared with her new fiancé.

Rebecca laughed. "Sorry, those days are over. Michael, this is the Jane I was talking about. Great kisser. I call her Dirty Jane because she wastes no time getting down and dirty."

"Well damn, I was hoping for a fling tonight." Crazy Jane took Rebecca's hand again, "But I can't compete with a rock like that. Or Michael's equipment, apparently. You too up for a three way?"

Our Jane was shocked in several different directions. Christian laughed. Jane thought, *Maybe I'm a prude after all.*

Michael seemed to be un-phased by anything. He smiled and said, "I'll let Rebecca field that request."

"He is *not* interested, Dirty Jane. Nice try," Rebecca pinched Jane's arm playfully.

Crazy Jane pivoted. "Can we at least stay and party? My new friends leave tomorrow, and they require a properly crazy night. Jane Walden here is a writer blowing off some steam."

"Walden? What are the odds of that? Two Jane Waldens at my house?"

Our Jane explained, "No coincidence. The book is about seven Jane Waldens. Same name, different lives. Oh, I should write that down for a tagline."

"Fabulous idea. I'd read that book. It almost sounds familiar. Oh, yeah! Like that documentary. Have you seen it? Anyway, now we have a theme for the party." Rebecca gestured like she was reading a marquee, "Welcome the Party of The Two Janes. Stay as long as you like. Michael here is flying me to a late dinner on Nantucket. We're taking a pre-honeymoon for a couple of days. He's a pilot, too. I love bragging about him."

"Okay, I really can't compete with that!" exclaimed Crazy Jane.

Rebecca hugged Jane again, Michael re-shook all hands, even Jesse's, and they were gone. Jesse made a beeline downstairs.

Our Jane processed something Rebecca said, "Did she say documentary?" She wanted to run after Rebecca, but it felt like the King and Queen and the procession had already left. *Great, something else to worry about,* she thought.

Christian caught the worry on her face, "Screw it, remember? Just stay in the moment. The book will be there tomorrow. I guess I'll go down now. You coming? Shit. I can't saw suggestive lines like that around you..."

"The joke's too easy. I'll be there in a minute," replied Our Jane, taking Christian's advice and focused on her surroundings. "I want to see the view. Craz... I mean Jane. Jane, will you give me the tour?"

Christian smiled. "Have fun. Remember, this is our crazy let-loose night. I'm not waiting for you to start the excessive drinking."

Crazy Jane said, "We'll start up here. Rebecca left us a lovely present." She pointed to the small table with several bottles of alcohol.

Our Jane smiled back at Christian. "I'll race you to drunk."

Christian went downstairs, leaving the two Janes alone on the widow's walk.

"What's the real story there?" Crazy Jane gestured toward the stairwell.

"You mean Christian?"

"Yeah, he's super geek-hot. Do you like him, or what?"

"I love Christian! He's been my best friend since I can remember. He's held my hands through a lot of shit."

"I don't know," Crazy Jane walked to the small bar table, "I'm getting a vibe."

A vibe went through our Jane for sure, but she knew it couldn't be jealousy. "Exercising your Bi status? He is single. Are you really interested? It seems like Christian's game for anything tonight." *Did I just give Crazy Jane permission to have sex with my best friend? I don't like where this is going, or how it feels. What is happening?*

"I don't know. Maybe I'm just picking up on his mood. I've got a good horny radar." Crazy Jane laughed. "Of course, it's wrong about half the time. Enough about him - buy you a drink?"

"Hell yes." *Good, let's steer away from Christian.* "After the pond, you have convinced me that this is not a day for holding back."

Crazy Jane poured two tall glasses nearly full of ice and clear liquor. Our Jane took a sip. "Straight Gin. You don't mess around girl."

"Nope." Crazy Jane clicked her glass as a toast. They walked around the widow's walk, watching the lights drift around the water and gazed at the twinkling lights in the sky. Crazy Jane told a more detailed version of the story of the Captain and his widow. How it had been a boarding house after the Captain's wife died, shared by three families in the early 1920's, before changing hands each decade as the values increased. The house was now worth over a million dollars and had been owned by Rebecca's parents since the 1990's.

They continued the tour with the bedrooms, down one flight of narrow stairs. The four doors they had seen on the second floor belonged to three bedrooms and a small bathroom, still in the style of a 1920's bathroom, complete with a flush box over the toilet.

None of the bedrooms were locked, but they only got to explore one. The other two were occupied by couples. The first one they checked contained a passed-out couple of young men, both half clothed. Crazy Jane shut of the tiffany style lamp, closing the door.

The other was occupied by a couple having strenuous intercourse, the girl on top and faced away from them. They were unusually quiet lovers. The room was fully lit, and they didn't stop their activity when the two Janes barged in. They closed the door on the people enjoying each other.

In the hallway, both Janes did not hide the laughter. Crazy Jane bent at the waist with laughter, spilling some Gin on the hard wood floor, her glass already nearly drained. They escaped into the unoccupied master bedroom,

It was larger than Jane expected, considering the other rooms. It helped that the bed was only a full size, and there were several noteworthy pieces of stunning antique furniture; a simple, but elegant armoire, and an expertly carved dressing table. Both looked to be early 18th century, probably wildly valuable. Jane knew few details, but was always drawn to antiques. She ran her hand over each piece of furniture, a tactile embrace.

There were also two stunning original artworks, both of the sea; one a seascape coastal scene, the other of a tall ship on an uneasy ocean. Heavy curtains draped the bay window, and a large freestanding full-length mirror stood in a corner. Two lamp tables flanked the bed, possibly genuine Tiffany.

Jane approached the mirror, sipping at her vanishing gin. To her surprise, she'd drained much of the glass, and was feeling more than buzzed. She had lost all track of time, and thought of Christian, who would probably be concerned she hadn't come down the stairs. Then she remembered how Christian behaved when he drank. Most people got silly, giddy, combative, or a mix. Christian got philosophical, and occasionally giggly. He'd probably found some college student, and was having a deep, drunk conversation about a minor 17th century French novel, or an obscure American revolutionary. He was likely making cogent points to the poor student, sounding more like a college professor, then suddenly giggling at his own point. Jane thought she heard the giggle even now.

Her sluggish mind came back to the now. In the mirror, over her shoulder, crazy Jane was naked. Jane watched Jane, watching Jane. Our Jane tried to snap back fully to reality, but the Gin didn't help. Crazy Jane went out of focus. For a moment, they were two blurs standing next to each other in the mirror. Two indecipherable, indistinguishable Janes. Her focus came back when she felt crazy Jane kiss the back of her neck, just off to the left side.

Crazy Jane's hands were on her stomach, laced fingers pulling her into her own naked body. She felt the warmth through her clothes and randomly got the image of Jane standing of her tippy toes to reach her neck with delicate lips.

Our Jane put her hands on Crazy Jane to unlace them. "No Jane. I'm sorry, but I don't want…"

Before she could finish Crazy Jane had spun her around and their lips met. She tasted the lip gloss, then Jane's tongue. She randomly thought of that old Katy Perry song, and wasn't sure if she liked kissing a girl or not.

She felt woozy, the room just beginning to spin. Then she kissed back, surprising herself. *Is this the booze? Do I want this?* Our Jane thought.

The word booze in her mind triggered something in her stomach. She pushed naked Jane away and nearly fell backwards into the mirror. She dropped her nearly empty glass to the throw rug, and staggered out the door for the only bathroom she knew of. The walls of the hallway were not cooperating and seemed to writhe under her unsteady arms. She felt like she was at sea, that the house was the ship in the painting. She made it to the bathroom just in time.

Gin burns like hell going both directions in the throat. Not to mention her dinner. She struggled to hold the bowl lid, and keep her hair out of the line of vomit. She retched for a second time, but it all had come out in the first go. She hadn't had time to close the door, so the sound must have carried to some parts of the house. She closed the door with her foot, awkwardly. It was an old-fashioned key lock, no way to secure it without a key. She hoped for a few minutes of privacy.

Jane finished at the bowl, washed her face, and rinsed out her mouth three times to get rid of the taste. She was still spinning, but less. Only some of the Gin had gotten into her blood stream. The towel felt cool against her mouth, so she splashed more cool water on her face. She felt better. Opening the door, she was startled by Christian's drunk giggle. He stood at the door, about to knock.

His laugh cut off when he saw her face. "You okay?" Christian slurred.

"Did you hear me throw up from down stairs?"

"You threw up? No, I was coming up to use the bathroom. Someone else was using the one down-stair... never mind. Are you okay?"

"Yeah, I think so." She unblocked the entrance to the bathroom, "You go ahead. I'll go downstairs with you after."

Christian used the bathroom, and Jane heard him talk to himself through the door. "Oops, no lock. Cool old keyhole."

Jane reluctantly peeked her head back into the bedroom. Would Crazy Jane be mad? Hurt? Ashamed at the rebuff? Jane was relieved to see her passed out on the bed, still unabashedly naked.

Christian was back in the hallway and peeked over her shoulder. "Wow. Hot," he said, still slurring and a little too loud. He pushed his glasses up. "Wait, did you two...?"

"No. She wanted to. We kissed, but that was it."

Crazy, drunk Jane didn't stir as they spoke. Our Jane went in and covered her up. She was surprised to hear a disappointed sound escape Christian as she covered up Naked Crazy Jane. She shook her head at Christian, who giggled again.

To her surprise, she had to help Christian down the narrow staircase. She was almost afraid he would pass out on the way down and they would both tumble.

They made it to a surprisingly vacant couch, after navigating through bodies on the floor. From the next room (dining room?) they heard Jesse speaking loudly, "Fucking Republicans. They screw up everything they touch. They should be banned everywhere."

This was met with giggles and spraying of laughter from whatever court Jesse was holding. "I mean it, man..."

Jane couldn't escape the smell, and saw the cloud billowing out from the small room. She'd never known pot to make anyone angrier. Luckily, Jesse and whoever was with him soon quieted down, the pot finally mellowing out Crazy Jane's prickly friend.

With so many passed out bodies strewn about, the room was warm with body heat. She and Christian started to drowse on the couch. Soon, they were both out for the night.

# Chapter 12

# To The Big City

"Life was a series of ironic ambushes." – Stephen King

Jane woke before Christian and found she was laying comfortably on his chest. It might have been romantic, she thought, but 1) it was just Christian, and 2) her drool on his shirt was anything but attractive.

She woke him up after wiping her mouth and was glad her purse was at her feet. She had no recollection of collecting her things, but she left it as another unanswerable mystery of the universe.

Christian woke slowly with a loud groan and held his head. "What did I drink last night?" he felt his shirt. "And why is my shirt wet?"

Jane replied, "Whatever you drank, you drank a whole lot of it. I threw most of mine up." She failed to give any theories on his wet shirt, hoping he had his own universal mysteries mental file.

"I remember a naked girl. Crazy Jane? I didn't... wait, did I?"

"No. Well, not that I know of." *Did I sneak back upstairs? Where was my purse before that?* She simply couldn't remember anything after getting to the couch. "You did see Jane naked upstairs. I'll explain later."

"What is that taste in my mouth?" Christian's face scrunched involuntarily. "Oh God, I drank absinthe. I remember now."

"I think we should go." *How many times have I been in Christian's shoes?* "I'll leave Jane a note. I doubt she's up yet." Jane looked around and was surprised to see less than half of the people that were present the night before. Almost like last night was a dream, slowly evaporating, people and all.

"Good idea. Back on the path," Christian said. "I hope I can stand."

He could, and Jane left a note that said –

*Sorry, had to leave. Thanks for everything. I'll let you know how the book goes. – The Other Jane.*

They walked on unreliable legs back to the harbor. Christian moaned a few more times, and was grateful when there was Advil at a small gift shop. It was a packet of two, overpriced, like the water bottle, but he gladly paid for some relief.

The first Ferry left for Boston at 6:30 am, so their timing was good. They left shortly, Christian quietly wishing his head would fall off, as Jane made notes about the day before. She started to made bullet points of the events of the day, but ended up writing about her feelings.

*I still don't know how I feel about the kiss. It could easily have led to more, and I think I was into it. I wish I could just blame the booze, which surely helped with inhibition lowering, but was it more than that? Was I just caught up in my own story? Her story? She clearly wanted me, was that part of why I wanted her? Would I have gone through with it?*

*I saw her naked twice yesterday. I was naked with her once at the pond. I didn't feel anything then. Am I overanalyzing this? Will any of this be in the book? Is this about my emotional journey, meeting these other versions of myself? Or maybe, I might be only a character in their chapters? I could make the emotional conclusion of what I've learned from their chapters, and save that conclusion for the last chapter, my chapter. Yes, I like that.*

Jane made copious notes, her thoughts spilling out in a way that hadn't happened on the trip yet. She felt on course, sure. The trek over water was 90 minutes. Jane remembered she needed to make a phone call, the last chance she'd get to confirm Christian's surprise. It looked like he was napping behind his sunglasses. Jane got her phone and moved to another part of the ferry.

She called, and confirmed the details. Jane hung up and told herself again it would be a great idea. Christian had done so much for her, helped her, that it was her turn to do the helping.

Jane checked her social media and email on the way back to Christian, annoyed that she still hadn't received a confirmation from New York Jane. In fact, she hadn't heard from her since leaving California. She would be forced to work on a back-up Jane on the way to New York.

Christian woke up just as they were pulling into Boston. The harbor was alive with activity. Ships and boats of all sizes filled the busy waterway. There were sails everywhere. Along with motor boats, tug boats, ferries, yachts, you name it.

They got off and began the trek back to their car. Christian was quiet most of the way, so Jane let her thoughts run on about the book, life, travel, and everything Jane. They arrived at the parking garage. Christian handed Jane the keys. "Sorry," he said, "I need to sleep for a while. Can you drive? The GPS is already programmed."

"Oh. Okay. No problem. I told you I'd drive anytime." She remembered the harrowing Boston experience, and the legendarily bad reputation of New York traffic. "I hope I don't kill us driving into New York City."

"You'll be fine," Christian said, and Jane wondered just how much the boy had drank after all. A weird vibe emanated from Christian, for sure.

She paid the nearly $40 for the 24-hour parking from the wallet Christian had left out between them. She smiled when she saw the faded picture of the two of them, just goofing off, sometime in the early college days.

Then, they were finally on the road headed to New York City.

The GPS very professionally told Jane to proceed onto the I-90 West and that the trip would take near four hours. Fate noticed Christian looked disheveled, wondering what fresh Hell Jane had put him through. Fate did her job professionally, and kept Jane on course. She hoped Jane would do the same for Christian.

Christian slept solid for over two hours. Jane felt surprisingly okay. She was lost in her thoughts about the night before, and the book in general. Worried over story structure again, she felt doubt creep back in, wondering for the billionth time if the main idea was captivating enough. They had passed by New Haven, Connecticut, slowed by an accident of some sort, when Christian bolted awake.

"I have to tell you something," he declared.

"Shit. Kind of startled me, kid." He'd winced when he came back to life, Jane noticed. "How's the head?"

Christian grabbed his noggin as though rediscovering it. "Still feels mushy and sharp at the same time. I don't know what I was thinking last night."

"A bit out of character," Jane flung him side eyes, "but it was nice to see you cut loose."

"Well, I'm paying for it now. We'll need to check into the hotel before I go sell my wares."

"Sell your wares? Only you could pull off that phrase. What did you need to tell me?"

Christian cleaned his glasses with his t-shirt. "You're not going to like it."

"That sounds ominous. What is it?"

He took a sigh, then blurted, "Dad didn't fund this trip. I did."

"What?" Jane jerked her head, and nearly swerved into the next lane.

"Eyes back on the road, please. Try not to freak out. I kept meaning to tell you. It was stupid not to. I'm only telling you now, because we really have to economize on the way back. The Hotel in New York is already paid for, and I have enough for food and gas, but we'll have to sleep in the car, or drive straight through after that."

"How could you not tell me this?" Janes head was racing around to ask the right questions. "Where did you get the money?"

"I had savings. This trip was important to you, and to help my Dad. My mom really screwed my dad in the divorce. They started the business together, so he still pays her. He won't tell me how much. Anyway, Dad couldn't afford this trip. He can barely afford to have me away this long. But now I've had some real sales. Well, a few anyway. With more along the way, we should be good."

"I am so mad at you right now!" Her mind raced, to figure out how she could help. "I have a little money left on my credit cards."

"You don't have 'money' left on your credit cards, Jane. You have some unused credit left. If you use that, you'll just be in more debt – on top of your student loans. And you're currently unemployed. I wanted to do this for you. And for my dad."

"Wow. This is a bomb shell. Maybe that's cliché, but that's what it is." She realized the emotional box she was in. "And I can't even be fully mad at you, because you're doing this for your dad and to help me. That's not fair." Her side eyes threw tiny daggers. "Your annoying nobility has just taken the wind out of my anger sails."

"Anger sails?"

"Hey, I want to be a writer. I can invent the occasional phrase."

Christian adjusted his freshly cleaned glasses. "I'm sorry I didn't tell you. As the trip went on, I didn't want to throw this complication into it. After last night, I think we need each other more than ever. I want to be there for you 100%."

"I appreciate the sentiment. I want to be there for you too." Jane meant it more than ever. "But what changed last night that made you want to tell me?"

"Hmm." Christian paused a long moment before he spoke. "I hope this comes out the right way. This book is a great idea. And it's an awesome dream to finally get a chance to complete. I've always supported your writing, you know that."

"Yes, you have," she smiled despite her anger. "That's one of the reasons I love you so much, my little Christian Jew."

"Still inappropriate, and incorrect. But let me continue: The danger of this time for you is that you are a little shaky after getting let go from the job, at the same time you are doing this very big thing. This thing which has a lot of facets to it. I'm afraid that you'll get lost in your own idea."

"Remember this was your idea." Jane considered. "Well, okay, our idea, I guess. Anyway, spit it out. You're dancing around it."

Christian looked meaningfully at Jane, "Well, you and Crazy Jane nearly had sex last night."

"Yeah. That was surprising."

"Not really. Well, yeah, surprising to me. I know you like men. Sure, it's a complicated sexual land-scape out there. I flirted with some gay stuff when I was younger. But I don't think it was that. I mean, let's face it – you nearly had sex with *yourself*."

"What?"

Christian grasped for the right words. "It's like you were living a metaphor for... I don't know... being too far in your own head. That's not it. Like, you were experimenting with a crazy version of yourself to see if you liked it. Sure, she's another person, but she's a stand-in for another part of your psyche."

Jane thought of seeing Crazy Jane in the antique mirror. "Like I stepped through a looking glass?"

"Maybe. More like you stepped into your own id, your own ego, or super-ego. I'm trying to remember psych class."

Jane needed a clearer picture. "A form of mastur-bation, you think?"

"Too simple. But, you are certainly in the deep wa-ters of this idea. I just don't want to see you get lost in it. Use it, sure. Crazy Jane will make for some good reading. Just find your way back out, you know?"

"And you'll be waiting for me when I do?" Jane gave another side-long glance, no daggers this time.

"Always."

"Okay. Warning taken, noted, and appreciated. Actually, I had a similar thought about this idea being like deep waters when we were in Wisconsin. Almost like you're reading my mind. Or that bitch fate at work again."

That made Christian laugh. The GPS glitched again and made a strange sound.

Jane said, "Thanks for being honest, old friend. Well, finally – about who paid for the trip, I mean."

There was a pause. Then Jane's tone changed, "Now tell me about this gay stuff."

"Oh no. What have I done?"

Jane probed, "Like gay sex? Gay porn stuff? What? Why were there no boy names on your sex list?"

Christian sighed audibly. There was no escape. "It was an *almost* experience that never happened after swimming at the pool. There was a moment, strange eye contact. Two half-naked teen guys. The awkward moment passed, nothing happened. End of story. I was just using it as an example of how we humans have weird sexual journeys."

"Well, that was disappointing." Jane narrowed her eyes, "I wanted red meat."

"You're incorrigible."

"Seriously, only you can get away with dialogue like that." Jane shook her head.

"You're not writing *this* into the book, are you?"

"You'll see when you read the first draft."

The GPS gave them directions for the inter-laced highway jogs they would have to do to get off the I-95 into Manhattan. They passed Port Chester and were now officially in New York State. As they got closer, the traffic intensified. The GPS did her job admirably, but Christian agreed to take over driving the last leg into the city. They stopped for gas, iced the beer samples, and were back on the road quickly.

Jane still hadn't heard from NY Jane, and was resuming her furious Google and Facebook searches for a quick replacement for Jane Walden #5.

"Still no luck?" asked Christian.

"No. In my mind, this is a lynchpin Jane for the book. I just have to have a New York Jane. There are only four in the city. Yeah, eight million people in the Big Apple, and only four Jane Waldens! I'm chiding myself for not nailing down two NY Janes to be certain. I've been too worried about…"

"About what?"

She thought, *your surprise*, but couldn't say that out loud. She messaged the other Jane that was on Facebook, hoping she'd get a reply in time.

"…about agents, of course." Jane checked her writer e-mail account again. Two new e-mails. "Yes! A reply from an agent." She read out loud, "Thank you for the interesting idea. Sounds like the documentary *Searching for Angela Shelton* and similar to *The Infinite Me*. Either way, it's not a good fit for our agency. Good luck in all your…blah, blah, blah."

"Documentary? Didn't that woman at the party…?" Christian said, leaving the concern out of his voice. "Better check it out – and do not freak out if..."

"Way ahead of you and I'm already freaking out. I knew I should have looked it up last night when that rich girl... Here it is. Listen to the synopsis. No wait, there's a trailer on YouTube...." Jane played the 2004 YouTube clip on her phone. The two-minute clip showed a woman named Angela driving around the country meeting other Angela Sheltons. To the filmmaker's surprise, 70% of them had experienced sexual abuse.

"Shiiiiiiiiiiiiiiittttttttttt!" Jane screamed.

"Now wait, just wait a minute. This is like the Joe Frank thing, the radio guy..."

"Christian! She interviewed forty other hers! Forty! Not a measly seven.... that's it. We're in New York, and I'm going to jump off the nearest bridge."

"No, you're not." Christian put his hand on Jane's arm. There was no hint of sarcasm or humor. "Jane. Your book is totally different. This filmmaker made a film about sexual abuse, with women that had her same name. We knew there might be intersecting themes, even this very idea..."

"She wrote a memoir, Christian." She showed her phone. She began to tear up. "It's right there on Amazon. Right there – a book about meeting other women with her same name. Shit. She even did a TED talk for NPR...."

"I see that. She told her story, and it ended up being about sexual abuse, and I'm sure a lot more. But this will be your story. Seven Ways to *Jane*. The book will be you, from all your glorious, well written angles. You can do this, Jane."

Jane blinked back her tears. "How do you do that?"

"Do what?" Christian realized he still held her arm, and put it back on the wheel.

"Bring me back from the edge like that, and make me feel like I can do anything?"

"It's not a chore, kid." He looked ahead and smiled, "Also, we have arrived."

Then came the skyline. They were still driving southbound into the city, so the famous skyline was different than the beauty shots in films, usually shot from the ocean in a helicopter. But it was still unmistakable from any angle. Jane and Christian both smiled at each other. Christian could only take his eyes off the road for a second as the traffic was already very heavy. But they shared the first-time-New-York-City-moment. Jane put a hand on Christian's shoulder and squeezed. Jane's doubts leapt off the proverbial bridge.

They passed the Botanical gardens, the Bronx Zoo, and then they were among the skyscrapers of Manhattan. They moved slowly and haltingly. If the traffic was bad, rude and infuriating in Boston, New York traffic was a new level of hell. Not only were there honkers and middle fingers flipped, but it was more traffic than Jane or Christian had seen anywhere. Los Angeles was a nightmare. This was Los Angeles's nightmare within a nightmare of what bad traffic could be like.

196

Since Christian had made the reservation, and most of the travelling details, Jane never asked the name of the New York Hotel where they would be staying. After the bombshell with Christian paying for everything, she knew it wasn't the Waldorf Astoria.

It was a beautiful old red brick building on a busy corner. They were in the West Village area. She tried to read the name of the hotel. The sign on the building simply read "Hotel." If there was a word above it, she couldn't read it from where they were. They parked, got their bags and walked into the lobby. An old-fashioned room greeted them, the bellhops in proper Hollywood-style bell-hop outfits and red bellman's caps.

When they got to the counter, the clerk said, "Welcome to The Jane."

"What?" Jane eyes grew wide. "Really?"

"Yep. On the corner of Jane street, no less. I thought it was fitting." Christian continued in a whisper, "Sorry it's not the Waldorf."

The clerk heard Christian, but didn't seem offended at the comparison. They were checked in, allowed the bell hop to take their bags up and Christian called dibs on the shower.

"We could shower together." suggested Jane in a deadpan.

"Don't start things you can't finish, young lady."

"Still into gay stuff, I understand." Jane said knowingly.

"I should never have told you."

"Nope."

"I'll be out soon."

"Out soon? That is too obvious a joke, even for me." Jane relented on the awkward jokes. "Your shower will give me time to make some more notes, then I take a quick shower and then our New York journey begins."

Christian started for the bathroom with his change of clothes.

Jane stopped him, "Hey, Christian?"

"Yeah?"

"Thanks for all this. The money, the support. The Jane Hotel. All of it."

"No problem. Maybe you'll be ready sooner than I thought."

"Huh?" Jane said, honestly baffled. "Ready for what?"

Christian almost said something serious, but changed it to a joke. "To take a shower with me someday, *obviously.*" Christian winked and disappeared into the bathroom.

Jane went over the timeline in her head while sitting on her matching double bed.

*1 PM – 3 PM, Sightseeing for me, sales calls for Christian.*

*3 PM - I (hopefully) meet up with NY Jane. Still no message from my back-up Jane. Poop, poop, and poop.*

*4 PM - Christian meets me at the same restaurant for the surprise. Depending on how that goes, dinner after. Then maybe a club? No, I don't want to waste any more of Christian's money. We'll just sight see free stuff together during the night. Then bed, up early to go to the last Jane in Biloxi.*

Jane made notes. *Maybe find a NY Jane after I get home? Perhaps a phone interview, or skype? Not the best scenario, since I'm actually here - New York. Here, now. But New York wouldn't be a total waste. Firstly, it was New York. Plus, Christian's surprise will be worth it.*

She briefly entertained a fantasy of walking into some high-powered New York Literary Agencies and insisting on seeing agents on the spot. She laughed as she imagined being dressed like Audrey Hepburn in *Breakfast at Tiffany's*. She excused the fantasy, but thought, *even I know that won't work, but New York is the place everything will click. I know it. It must.*

The shower went off, and in only a few minutes, Christian was dressed and out of the bathroom.

"Guys - shower, comb your hair and done."

"Not this again. A lot of people are jealous that I have a dick."

"A lot of people think you *are* a dick. Like me. Right now," Jane punctuated this by a very mature sticking out of her tongue in Christian's general direction.

He smiled defiantly.

When they were both ready, they drove to a general area around the restaurant Jane had picked. It was a spot not too far from Tiffany's flagship store. It was one of the sights she had on her list. She couldn't have breakfast at Tiffany's like the famous novella, since there was no restaurant attached. It was just a metaphor, anyway. But she could visit there on her stroll, and stand where Audrey Hepburn had stood in the movie, eating a danish and gazing in the window at the lifestyle she coveted but would never afford. Jane could at least do that.

Christian said, "You know, you could come along for a sales call or two if you want."

"Oh. Yeah. Okay. Let's do that. I won't bring up any of the gay stuff in front of your clients."

"This is going to be a thing now, isn't it?"

"Yep."

All the horror stories of traffic in New York were true, cliché reaffirmed, as they drove the Manhattan streets. They ended up triangulating a parking structure near two beer & wine distribution companies where Christian was going to try to "sell his wares." Parking was awkward, and they were surprised to find parking worked very differently from California to New York. They were also surprised at the stiff parking tax.

The car settled, they went to their first stop. Simply called Five Boroughs Distributing, it was run by an old man named Nick who was clearly tired and angry. This was a cold call, not one of Christian's appointments. Nick actually laughed when he heard the phrase "California Micro Brew." He did all but throw them out.

Back up at street level, Jane asked, "Have there been a lot of guys like that?"

Christian shrugged, "A few."

"That sucks. I didn't know selling beer would get you mock and scorn."

"One guy brought out a baseball bat and just eyed me. Didn't look at the bat, just stared me down."

Jane blanched, "Holy shit. Where was this?"

"Wisconsin. It was my fault. Everyone else there was great, but I chose the wrong cold call. I should have noticed the wall sign faster. It read: 'If it ain't from Wisconsin, it ain't beer.' Don't worry, the next one is an appointment."

The appointment was at a slick operation called Proud Union Beer Company. They entered into the warehouse, not sure where the front office entrance was kept. Very clean and bustling. A worker in a hard hat pointed the way to the office, indicating he'd alert the boss. They found the small office, also very neat, when the boss arrived.

"Shit. Was that today?" Boss Johnathan said. "Sorry. I got my acquisitions director out sick with her kid. She does all my buying."

Christian said in a cool, relaxed voice, "That's okay. Can I set up a tasting for you, leave a card? Or maybe, just leave a few samples? She can call me if she likes them."

Jane had never seen Christian in salesman mode. He was more confident that she expected. A long way for the nerdy English Major, who could seemingly give his opinion of every major work of fiction from the last five hundred years.

"Sure. I'll take a few samples and a card. I'm a Vodka and Bourbon kind of guy. She's the beer expert, that's why I hired her. Sorry for the mix up. Thanks for coming out."

"No worries. Here you go." Christian expertly handed off a few samples and a couple of cards.

Outside, Jane said, "This trip must be so stressful for you, all the rejection. I should have realized what you were going through. I guess we're both setting up for rejection."

"I will admit, the trip has not been as successful as I hoped. Dad has been impressed by the sales I've made, but... well, I know the numbers. There's a break-even point for this idea. I'm not quite there yet. I don't want to let Dad down."

"Time for me to be the cheering squad," she punched Christian in the arm. "You can do this, kid. You make me proud! Crap, that was mediocre. I need to get better at this."

Christian smiled. "I've still got five more appointments, and I'm going to do a few more cold calls after that. You ready to explore the city on your own for a while?"

"Yes!" Jane glanced at the rolling ice chest of samples. "But I'd be happy to go on more appointments with you."

"Nah. It's cool. It's boring to watch." Christian looked down at the cooler. "It's pretty boring to do, but I'll keep plugging away."

"If you're sure." Jane reassured, "I won't explore the entire city without you. I'll save some for tonight."

"Sounds good." said Christian, "Still on for 4 PM to meet New York Jane? You sure you need me there?"

It was the first time Jane felt a pang of regret. She tried never to lie to Christian. She answered, "Of course. I think it's important you meet her. 4 o'clock sharp, mister. We're going to have an awesome time. I know it." She still didn't come clean that she would be done with Jane by then (if she showed), and 4 PM was his surprise.

Christian gave her a dubious look, but agreed. They temporarily parted ways. Jane was now in New York, New York - Manhattan Island. Only blocks from Central Park, she was right in the heart of mid-town. She passed the stylish sculptured "Love" sign, near 6th avenue. She quickly understood just how big city blocks were in New York City. It didn't matter; the city streets flew by with her excitement. *Too bad it's only one day in New York*, she thought, but she was determined to see all that time would allow.

Jane started walking east, toward 7th Avenue, but was disappointed by the lack of sights. Lots of tall buildings with businesses along the way, but little else, so she turned the corner and headed back toward 5th Avenue. She didn't want to be the tourist with her face planted in her phone, so she only referred to Google Maps to make sure she was headed straight for NY eye candy.

She saw the Gucci sign and paused before entering. She knew she could never afford anything, but she took the plunge and went inside. After seeing some beautiful things, she checked her watch. It was already after two, and NY Jane was (supposed) to be a few blocks away at 3 PM. She'd found no fill-in Jane, and was 99% sure NY Jane would be a no show. She mentally kicked herself for letting that happen, but still, she was in New York. She hurried around the corner to Tiffany's.

Jane stared blankly up at the modern building. All reflective surfaces, she saw the name TRUMP. She hadn't noticed on her phone that Tiffany's was located in Trump Tower. A swirl of emotions threatened to overtake the moment, so she purposefully shut out any political thoughts. She focused on the story of the moment, and stared at the sign. With elegant green awnings, it announced "Tiffany & Co."

Jane hadn't seen Breakfast at Tiffany's for a while, so she Googled the scene to try and stand at the very same spot Audrey Hepburn had. She positioned herself just outside the window, staring in, just as the actress had done.

She felt... nothing. No connection to that famous moment, no connection to the shop, no harkening to Holly Golightly's story of a girl lost in New York, trying to find herself. *Strange. I thought this moment would feel different.* Something about that thought made her stomach churn. She was glad she hadn't brought a danish and coffee, like in the movie. Jane brushed aside the disappointment. This was New York, dammit.

Jane realized she was hungry. She'd get a little something at the restaurant, before NY Jane (maybe) arrived. She left her surprisingly empty moment and walked on to the restaurant. Rue 55 was a French and Sushi restaurant. *What could be more melting pot than that, in this great American city?* She'd made reservations long ago to accommodate NY Jane and Christian's surprise.

Our Jane arrived at 2:45 and was seated promptly. She'd chosen it not just for the variety, but the fact that it had a two $$ menu. Which, she found, in Manhattan meant that they were equivalent to four $$$$ prices elsewhere. It was a long way from Wisconsin cheese curds, and mid-west prices.

The place was small, but elegant, with classic white tablecloths. It felt warm and inviting. There was outdoor seating, which seemed very New York to Jane, but she opted for the cozy interior.

As she feared, New York Jane never showed.

She ordered some Pomm frites, and a lemonade. When she realized NY Jane wouldn't show, she gave into the urge for French onion soup. Ironically, not the best she'd had. At twenty minutes until four, and the big surprise, she indulged in a glass of French wine. Ten minutes until four, a woman stood over her table.

# Chapter 13

# The Surprise

"Experience is the name everyone gives to their mistakes."
– Unknown

"Three dilemmas make a crisis." – Jonathan Katz

"Pardon me? Are you Jane Walden?" The woman was about fifty, but looked much younger. She wore expensive black jeans, tall black boots, and was layered in an earth tone sweater. Her neck was wrapped in a billowing scarf, and she wore oversized sunglasses. The woman was thin, and she almost didn't recognize her from the few pictures Jane had seen of her in younger days.

Jane stood up and extended her hand. "Mrs. Jacobson?"

"Oh, no. It's Robinson. I changed it back to my maiden name. Please, call me Bobbi."

"Oh, I thought you first name was Teresa."

"It is. My middle name is Barbara. When I divorced Christian's dad, my new self wanted to be called Bobbi. It's how New York knows me."

"Well, thank you for coming," Jane invited her to sit. "and early."

"Oh yes. Living in New York, you never know what's going to slow you down. I leave early for everything."

"I wish I had that habit. Still working on it. Christian's always on time. Must get that from you." An indefinable awkwardness hung between them. Jane tried to power through it. "Anyway, thanks for meeting us. Christian will be here shortly."

"I'm surprised he wanted to see me. He never calls. Not even a text." Bobbi's eyes were piercing. "Do you know what he want to see me about?"

"Oh, umm. I think he just wants to re-connect, you know."

Bobbi finally removed her sunglasses as she finally sat. "Why?"

"Why?" The word struck a discordant note, like an unpleasant sound in a horror film. Jane didn't know how to respond. "I mean, he's your son. Does he need a reason?" Jane laughed, but it came out forced and awkward. She stammered, "I... I don't want to put words in his mouth, of course. From my point of view, as his best friend, I think he's kind of stuck when it comes to women. He never seems to have a girlfriend very long. Maybe he needs to work on his relationship with you." Jane had not meant to over-share her theory, nerves just made it dribble out.

"That's not what we talked about on the phone." She looked at her watch, visibly irritated. "I really don't have time for a therapy session. If he has trouble with women, maybe he should see a doctor. Maybe he inherited his father's tiny penis, or Frank's low testosterone. I didn't come here to fix my son."

Jane was searching for words, but none came. She glanced at her watch and it was one minute until four. Jane had imagined at best, a tearful reunion of mother and son, at worse, an icy beginning that warmed... to a tearful reunion between mother and son. Now, the cheese from the French onion soup sat in the pit of her stomach and began to ache. This was clearly a mistake. Jane had to stop this. She stood.

Then she saw Christian.

Jane stood, facing Christian coming toward the table. He had already seen her and was headed their way. His mother was seated, her back to him. He came around the table. Jane was frozen on the spot. She couldn't think of any way to stop it.

Christian began speaking before he'd made the turn around the table, sounding like he was still in salesman mode. "Hello. This must be the other famous Jane Walden..." He'd been slowly extending his arm while he walked around. Seeing his mother, his arm dropped to his side like a dead thing.

"What the hell is she doing here?" Christian said, staring at his mother, but talking to Jane.

"Hello, son." Bobbi ignored the tone and asked, "What did you want to talk about?"

"Christian. I...." Jane's mouth was desert dry. Words finally fell out. "This was supposed to be a surprise..."

"I'm surprised," he crossed his arms, still standing, staring down his mother.

Jane remarked, "I can see that. So am I, after meeting your mother. I didn't think... anyway, I'm babbling. Umm. okay. Maybe we could just sit down?"

"This is what you've been spending all of dad's money on?" He indicated her clothing. "A New York lifestyle with designer shit hanging off you, like no one will notice you're over fifty?"

"Passive-aggressive anger with snarky comments." Bobbi smiled wanly, "Wonder where you got that from?"

"No passive here. All aggressive."

Jane tried again, "Maybe we could sit down."

"Yes, son. Sit down. Let's chat. I only have a little while anyway; another appointment."

"What in God's name would I want to talk to you about?" Christian still had not sat down.

"We haven't seen each other in over ten years," Bobbi said icily. "We could talk about that."

"Why?"

"I have no idea," she checked her watch again. "The thought had crossed my mind that your little friend here set this up, pretending you wanted to talk. I dismissed it as B movie nonsense. But here we are."

Jane said, "I am so sorry..."

Bobbi put her hand up, imperiously stopping Jane, unconcerned that she had been apologizing to Christian. "But your little friend there took a lot of time and energy to set this up. I hear you're having trouble with the ladies. We could talk about that."

Christian moved his head to slowly stare at Jane. "Can you please tell me exactly what you told her?"

Jane reeled to remember the words. She hesitated, but couldn't think of anything but the truth. "I... I said I wondered if your problems with long term relationships maybe had something to do with *not* having a relationship with your mother."

"I know why I have trouble with long term commitments." He still spoke to Jane. He jerked a thumb toward his mother as he finally sat down, "And it has nothing to do with that woman."

Bobbi cocked her head back and let out a laugh. It was not pleasant. "My God, Christian, you are so dramatic. Just like your father. I left him years ago, and I'd do it again. I am sorry I hurt you, but let's be honest, we've never really liked each other. We were just two people surviving the same bad idea."

Christian stared at the table, refusing to meet her eyes again. "Don't talk about Dad. Only warning."

Bobbi changed her tack. "You can't say I never called you, never sent gifts."

"You called me exactly three times since I was Eleven. I stopped receiving gifts from you when I was fifteen."

"That's because you sent them back to me. I know it wasn't your father, because they always came back with a very terse note from you. I wasn't going to force myself into your life if you didn't want that. You're just like your father, anyway. You had a better life there with him, what could I offer? I can say a lot of sad, pathetic things about him, but he was always a good father."

"How generous of you." Christian still hadn't reestablished eye contact with his mother.

"My God, this was such a mistake," Jane whispered to herself.

Christian heard her. "Yes, it really was, Jane." He took a deep breath and held it for a long time. Jane watched his mouth with some alarm. Finally, some red washed away from his face and he released the breath. "But I see why you did it."

"That's interesting. Why aren't you furious at her...?" Bobbi looked back and forth between Christian and Jane. She began to laugh again. Bobbi threw her head back and did not attempt to restrain herself. The discordant sound boomed through the small restaurant. "Oh, my God! You love this girl. That's it, isn't it? You're having problems with woman because you want Jane!"

Her laughter whizzed around the restaurant. The patrons that hadn't been paying attention before, all stared at them now. "My God. Son, if there's one thing you can learn from me is go get what you want. She's right there. She obviously loves you on some level, since she arranged this," she raised the palms of her hands like this event was born to be mocked. "Honestly, I never loved your father. I thought I did, but when I realized I didn't, I could no longer live that plebian life with a struggling small business. No security. Money sometimes, sell everything the next year. No pension, no savings. Always the smell of stale beer. It was time to get out. Frank is better off without..."

Christian shot out of his chair, and in one fluid motion the glass of lemon water was in his hand, and the contents doused Bobbi's expensive makeup and outfit. The thin slice of lemon stuck to her cheek. Bobbi didn't speak.

"You don't get to say his name," he went around the table and leaned in right next to his mother's shocked, wet face, "ever."

Christian stormed out.

Jane bolted out of her chair to follow him. She grabbed her purse, and awkwardly realized she still had to pay the bill. She couldn't be near that woman anymore. She almost said sorry to her, but couldn't bring herself to do it. Bobbi let Jane off the hook. "It's okay. I deserve it," she wiped her face of the water, picking off the lemon slice with here elegantly manicured nails. She stared at her wilting scarf. With an emotion Jane could not fathom, Bobbi said, "I deserve a lot of things. Just go."

She found the server and paid the bill, which seemed to take a painfully long time. Bobbi still hadn't left her seat. She just sat there, not attempting to dry herself further.

Jane left and ran out the door. She was afraid she'd lost Christian. There was a lot of foot traffic. She scanned both ways, and was sure she spotted him going north on 5th Avenue. She guessed where he was going.

She finally confirmed it was him, far down the street. He was walking much faster than her. *At a storm's pace*, her writer mind thought. Her flats were comfortable, but not made for fast walks. It was four city blocks until she caught him just at the edge of Central Park. Crossing 59th Street, she called out, "Christian, please stop!"

He didn't turn around, but he slowed and finally paused at the edge of the park. He slid his hands in his pockets and waited. She finally reached him and forcibly hugged him. "I'm so sorry, Christian. I had no idea."

"Why, Jane? Why did you have *no idea* what she's like? I never said anything good about her."

"No, you never said anything about her at all." It was not time to indicate this was Christian's fault in any way. Jane was so sorry, she didn't know where to begin. "It's the one place you never let me in. But, my God, I couldn't know that she was..."

"... a monster? Well, she is. A self-centered, egotistical, trying-desperately-to-keep-hold-of-her-youth succubus." Christian finished.

"I see that now." Jane still clung to him.

Christian finally hugged back. "I know what you were trying to do. I get it. But that was a huge mistake, Jane."

"I know. I'm so sorry you have *that* for a mother. I thought my sister was bad. But holy shit, Christian."

He managed a half smile. "Boy, did she mess up Dad. It hurt at the time, but I'm glad she left when she did. Image what she could have twisted inside him if she stayed for another decade." Christian's voice remained steel, impenetrable. "I have no illusions about her. Never did, really. Just because you're related by fate, doesn't mean you can't walk away. After today, I never have to see her again."

"Normally I'd say that's sad." Jane hugged him tighter. "But really, she is just totally awful."

That got a chuckle out of Christian. His laughing made Jane laugh, and soon the laughter peeled. New Yorkers might have thought them insane, but, well, it was New York. It tapered off, and they began strolling through Central Park.

As they strolled, Christian asked, "Any more surprises I should know about?"

"No! God, no. I promise. But we have to talk about what she said…"

"No. Please, Jane. I… can't discuss anything that came out of that woman's mouth. Not now." Christian stopped. With alarm, Jane saw that he was on the verge of tears.

She couldn't remember ever seeing him cry. *But I can't just drop what she said.* She looked as Christian turned away to wipe his eyes. *I've already put him through that scene. It will have to wait.* Jane smiled widely, and spread her arms. "Hey, buddy. Look where we are. We're in Central friggin' Park!"

Christian turned back and smiled. Apparently, that was the last tear for Bobbi. "Why yes, yes we are. What are we going to do about it?"

They took the necessary selfie. Jane held out her arm. "Would you be so kind as to take my arm, good sir?"

"That was kind of a southern accent you slipped into, and this is New York. Get it straight, kid. And, yes, you may take my arm, young lady."

"We only have tonight." Jane said excitedly, "Maybe - we should do a montage of all the fun things we want to do in our one day in the Big Apple. What do you say?"

"As long as we can walk there." Christian shook his head. "Driving in this city is a fucking nightmare."

"We'll do that. We'll walk, take a city bus. Ooooh! The subway."

"Let's shoot the works – on the cheap, that is." Christian laughed softly. "Today, *you* are the New York Jane. Let's do it."

A montage is exactly how it felt. They walked for miles, got a bus when Jane's shoes began hurting, took a subway, saw a few New York bums, got hot dogs, and slowly the lights came alive in the city. Since they both agreed this was a literary journey as well, they stopped by the New York Public Library. Christian would have stayed there all night if Jane had let him. They walked arm in arm sometimes, other moments they raced up streets for no reason at all, giddy in the moment. It was a magical night in the big city.

Little did they know what storm fate would bring them that night.

# Chapter 14

# Yes

"A whale, a gale, some intelligent destroyer." –
Herman Melville

"Truth is a mortal blow." – Neil Finn

They finally got back to their Jane hotel, sometime after midnight. Physically and emotionally, they were both exhausted. Back in the room, they got ready for bed. Jane let Christian use the bathroom first, since he took so little time, and Jane did her usual routine, finally done by 1 am.

Under the blankets, Christian's eyes were already closed when she got out of the bathroom. His bed side lamp was out. She crawled into her own bed, put the light out. She lay there for a while before she said, "What time do we leave tomorrow?"

"Check out is 11 am. I'm thinking breakfast at nine, leave by ten. That okay? Biloxi is about 19 hours away, driving straight through. Leave here by 10, get to Mississippi by 6 am the day after. Be a long haul, but you said that Mississippi Jane is flexible with her schedule, right?"

"Yeah, retired. She said anytime. I'll call her the night before. Hey, maybe she'll let us use her shower after 19 hours on the road."

Christian chuckled drowsily, "Yeah, maybe."

Silence. Then Jane said softly, "You know we have to talk about it."

"We've been talking all night." Christian sounded as though he was already drifting off.

"About what your mother said." small pause. "Your mother thinks you love me."

Long pause. "She thinks a lot of things. Go to sleep."

"You're evading."

A sigh in the dark. "I don't have wide experience with the ladies, true. But why do women want to have serious discussions right before men fall asleep?"

"Still evading." Jane pushed. "Why would your mother say that? She doesn't know either of us."

"She's a crazy monster," Christian said. "Don't pay any attention to her."

Another long pause.

"Christian, is it true?"

The longest pause of all.

"Yes."

Jane turned on her lamp. She bolted out of bed and ran to the end of his bed. She stubbed her toe on his bed frame. "Owww!"

Christian turned on his lamp. "Are you okay?"

"No, damn it. I stubbed my toe!"

"Is it broken?" He got out of bed, in his pajama bottoms. Jane sat on the edge of his bed. He examined her toe. "Try to wiggle it. Yeah. It's okay. Just a stub. You'll be fine."

"Fine? FINE?" Jane realized her pitch was rising. "How could you not tell me?"

Christian withdrew from Jane and stood up. "I shouldn't have to tell you at all."

"What?" Jane cocked her head. "What the hell does that mean? Why?"

"Jane, I've been in love with you since... forever. I've tried to be with other girls, but they're never you."

"Oh, Christian. Don't..."

"It's not my mother that's holding me back. It's you. It's always been you."

"Christian... I don't know what to say."

"It's okay." Christian rubbed his head and reached for his glasses. "I didn't tell you because you're still not ready."

"Wait..." Jane stood and put her hands on her hips, "what?"

"We're the same age, but you still have some growing up to do." Christian paused. "No, that came out wrong..."

"Bet your ass it did. So, what... I'm not good enough for you, *yet*? Is that what you're saying?"

"No." Christian struggled. "No, I mean you haven't realized that you love me too."

"What? What? No, no, no. You're actually telling me I'm such a bubble headed idiot that I haven't noticed the guy who *I thought* was my best friend is secretly in love with me? How am I supposed to know that? Psychic powers?"

"This is not coming out right..." Christian rubbed the back of his head. "Look, what I mean is that..."

"That I'm not mature enough for you?" Jane crossed her arms.

"No. No, Jane, dammit!" Christian bolted up. "That you don't know me at all. My last name is Jacobson. You know that old joke about me being your Jewish Christian? Well, firstly it's never been funny, and it's always mildly offensive. And secondly, Jacobson is an old English name. It literally means son of Jacob."

"How the hell am I supposed to know that?" Jane threw up her hands. They landed back on her hips.

"Because I've told you like 600 times!"

"You have not!"

"I have, Jane." Christian took a step forward. "I really have. You just keep *not* hearing me because you're so wrapped up in yourself." Christian took a step back after the last bit came out all wrong, as well.

"Excuse me?" Jane closed in a few steps. "So now I'm selfish? Or just self-centered? Which is it?"

Christian stood his ground. "A little of both, actually."

"Well, screw you, buddy. Selfish? Who's the best friend that never would let me in – never would explain what his mother was like? You, old pal." Jane began to pace. "Wait, wait... All those times I cried on your shoulder about some guy, you weren't being objective." Memories flooded, realizations clicked. "Oh, my God! All those times you told me a guy was a jerk, you had other motives!"

"No. Jane, you do have terrible taste in men. You *have* dated a lot of objectively, factual jerks – and you know it!"

"How am I to know the real reason? How can I trust anything you say?" A big intake of air. "Holy shit, you've been lying to me all this time!"

"No Jane. No. Not telling you this doesn't mean I was lying. I've just been waiting..."

"Lying by omission!" yelled Jane. "Why do guys always think that doesn't count? And for what, Christian? For what? How does your script end? Jane suddenly grows a brain, and sees her 'one true love' has been right there, patiently waiting?" Another nuclear bomb went off in her mind. "Oh my God... is that what this *trip* is about?"

"No, Jane. Damn it. Stop. Please. This trip was about finding yourself. Finally. This is supposed to be a cathartic experience where you find the real Jane."

"The real Jane? The real Jane?" She noticed she was repeating herself, she couldn't help it. "Which one is that? Which one? The one that's madly in love with a dope that doesn't have the balls to tell me he loves me?"

Christian rushed up to Jane and kissed her.

Jane pulled back and slapped Christian across the face. "How. dare. you."

She paced. Christian stood, frozen in his hot lips pajama bottoms.

Jane muttered, "I don't even know who you are. I've been hanging out with a total stranger."

"That's right, Jane. You don't know me! You've never tried to know me at all." Christian's anger finally showed up, "How dare *you* set a trap with my *mother* – behind my back! Lying by omission? You're guilty too. That proves you don't know me at all! What were you thinking?"

"I... I was thinking of you! That you could finally find the right girl after you faced you mother."

"Well, great job." He indicated their current scene. "Look how well that turned out!"

"I've already apologized for that." Tears threatened. It made Jane angrier.

Christian lowered the verbal temperature. "And I accept that. But it illustrates the point that you're not ready to accept *how much* I love you. You have to see the real me standing here. It won't work any other way. I'm ready for you. I haven't been hiding. But until you can see me, we can't be true partners in love. If you can't see yourself, how will you ever see me?"

"Who talks like that?" Jane said, "I don't know you? I'm not sure I want to know you. Not after..."

"Don't be ridiculous. We are meant to be together." Christian had rehearsed a version of this conversation to himself for years. In his anger, the words felt like a foreign language. "I've been modulating the obvious – to give you time to see the, oh hell, the plot device, I guess. Here it is. The reveal – but you still can't see it. You're still not ready."

"My God, that's pretentious, even for you!" Jane wasn't finding the right words either. The anger clouded everything. "What did you say before... Partners in love? Really?" For some reason, the phrase offended her. "Who are you? You're right, I don't see you. I don't know who the hell you are. No, no, no. I can't do this."

"What? No, no Jane. Jane, stop. Please."

Jane suddenly stopped and sucked air, another realization. She looked around the room like it was all new to her. "A trap. That's what this is. You got me all alone, all the way across country. No way out... so what, I'd *have* to love you? I have to see this *'truth'*?"

"I'm sorry. Jane, Jane, Let's talk..."

"Talk?!" The full storm had arrived, along with the tears. "About what? That you're a liar? That you've been trying to pull my strings – for me to come to some realization that you're the perfect man for me? How dare you think so little of me. Maybe you don't know *me* at all! Ever think of that?" Jane's breath caught in her throat. Something had crashed, broken, smashed. The tears gushed. Jane felt like she was in someone else's body. It wasn't dizziness. It was decision. She realized she couldn't be near Christian any more. "I... I have to go."

"What? What do you mean? Go where?" Panic rose in Christian, and the words just fell out, "Jane, don't be stupid..."

"There it is!" The fresh tears mixed with rage. "That's the real you. The Christian that thinks Jane is too stupid to see how *you* feel."

"Jane, I... please, Jane..."

"This trip is over. You can drive back. I don't... I don't think I ever want to see you again. I'll fly home."

"Jane, please. No, please." Christian tripped over every word. He grasped for what had been lost. "Let's just forget this. We were so close, almost asleep. To-morrow is a fresh, new day. We'll go back to the way it was."

Jane gathered her things and shoved them in her suitcase. "Now who's being stupid? We can't go back from this. I know I'm over-reacting. Right here in this moment, I know it. You think I don't know I'm a handful? I do. But this? I can never un-know this, Christi..." But she couldn't even say his name now. She stared at him, new tears in her eyes. "How could you do this? I do love you, Christian. You're my friend, my rock, my fucking soul mate. But now we can never be together. I feel just as betrayed now as every jerk that cheated on me. And it's my Christian that did it. You ruined everything."

"Please, Jane. I love you."

Those words had never felt so painful.

She stopped at the door, but had no strength to look at his face. "I loved you too, Christian. I'm sorry my love wasn't the specific kind you needed." She

224

looked around for anything she'd forgotten. "Good-bye Christian."

Jane left.

Christian wanted to go after her. Dying to go after her, to fix it. He stood dazed, unmoving. Indecision froze him to the spot. Of all the scenarios he'd imagined, losing Jane was never one of them. He didn't want to make things worse. He wasn't sure if they could get any worse. Having no idea of time, he finally ran down the stairs, out the lobby in his pajama bottoms and bare feet.

The cab was just pulling away with Jane. He could only see the back of her head. Christian waited in the cold night for a long while. He half expected a sudden rain, just like in the movies. He stood on the street, every muscle aching from the scene upstairs. The cab didn't return.

Fate had taken Jane away.

# Chapter 15

# Explosions

"Failure is not a crime. Failure to learn from failure
is."
– Walter Wriston

Jane arrived at the airport after 2 am. She'd cried
the entire cab ride, probably freaking out the cabbie.
Then again, she reasoned he was a New Yorker. He'd
probably seen it all. Jane ignored the three calls, and
twelve texts from Christian.

On the way, she'd checked on her phone to see the
rates for a one-way flight back to California. She had
enough room on her credit cards to swing the fair,
with enough left over to get her all the way home.
Then she thought about the book. *This is all I have
now.*

She booked a one-way flight to Biloxi. From there,
the rates were pretty cheap to get another one to Cali.
She would still be one Jane short. *Of all the stops to go*

*so badly, it had to be New York, didn't it?* She would go through with the plan to interview a New York Jane remotely. Jane was pretty sure it would be a long time until she came back to the Big Apple. She'd have lots of time to make notes, since her flight didn't leave for another eight hours; she'd booked what she could afford, forcing her to fly out of La Guardia airport. According to Mr. Internet, La Guardia was notorious for delays. *What choice do I have?* She mentally prepared for a long wait.

Just before the security line, she got another text from Christian. He was at the airport. Perhaps ironically, at JFK - the wrong one. In the same city, they were far apart in every way possible. It may have been symbolic, or some other analogy. Or fucking fate, again. Jane was in no mood for story constructs. She was so angry at Christian, the man that would never be *her* Christian ever again. Not the way he wanted, not the way she wanted. That was over, dead, gone.

Jane texted back that it was too late, that she had a non-refundable ticket (which was true). She didn't even tell him he was at the wrong airport. *Just go home Christian. Go home.*

She decided to rest a few terminals away from where her flight would depart. It might not be safe to sleep alone, even behind the TSA security. She slept anyway. Her phone alarm reached her from bad dreams that she couldn't remember. Jane was pretty sure what they had been about, anyway. The purse and laptop were still next to her. There were a lot more people in the airport, but no one bothered her.

Getting coffee, she checked the departure board. Her flight was delayed, over ten more hours. *What the hell? I'll be here forever.* Jane checked with a very busy clerk. A lot of people were angry about the ridiculous delays, but the clerk confirmed the truth of it with a cool, professional smile. 18 hours in an airport. Jane remembered the Purgatory bar, and now understood New York was her hell.

She had a weak moment and called The Jane Hotel. Christian had checked out. He was gone. Back to California. Of course he was. Jane felt anger swell again, but it was anger at herself for having a moment of weakness, and felt sad about Christian being gone. She felt completely alone.

Coffee and a danish in hand, she thought of *Breakfast at Tiffany's*. It brought a smile, but a sad one. The whole trip now meant so many new things. So many memories rang false now. Jane got freshly angry at Christian, at the betrayal. Yet other emotions swirled – *he loves me. How the hell do I feel about that?* She needed to escape. She needed fiction-therapy. Jane wandered through a book and magazine shop close to her terminal. She might explore the whole airport by the time her long-delayed flight starting boarding.

A book caught her eye: *The Infinite Me.*

She scrambled for her phone, juggling her danish and coffee. She went into her e-mail and scrolled to find a specific rejection e-mail.

*. . . Sounds like the documentary* Searching for Angela Shelton. *And similar to* The Infinite Me.

Jane had been distracted by the Angela Shelton documentary. She'd been meaning to look *The Infinite Me* up on Amazon, but it was right before New York, and Christian's mom-surprise. It had been a busy day of her life falling apart. She had forgotten about the book.

Dropping her things, she reached for the book. It was in hardback, so she looked at the inside dusk jacket for the description.

*The Infinite Me, a novel, by Joan Jamison.*

*Joan is a middle-aged woman who has never found herself. One day while "ego surfing" her own name online, she realizes there are a lot of other women with her name. Joan embarks on a journey of self-discovery as she connects with these other women, all named Joan Jamison. Through the lives she shares, the stories she experiences, Joan finds the community she has been searching for, and maybe finds herself along the way.*

*Oh no,* thought Jane, *it's happened. Someone else wrote my book.*

*No, no, no, no, no.* The word kept rolling through her mind. As a man perused the magazines near her, she realized she was saying it out loud. "No, no, no. . ."

*I have to tell Christian. Oh no, I can't. I can't tell my best friend. I've lost him. I've lost my Christian.*

She'd been holding the book open. The pressure had bent the front cover. She bought the book, forgetting her coffee and danish on a nearby shelf. She checked her watch and the departure board. She still had many hours until her flight took off. *My flight? What's the point now?* she thought. Then she remembered her ticket was non-refundable. She would have to go through with the Biloxi trip.

Finding a chair near an outlet, Jane let her laptop and phone charge. She dug into the book. Unlike Our Jane's almost-book, it wasn't a road trip diary, but a novel. The novelist used her own name as the lead character. The introduction explained that although she got the idea from ego surfing her own name, she began to fictionalize her research and interviews. There was also a love story element where a high school sweetheart had married a different Joan Jamison. Jane thought this plot point was too far-fetched, but she was holding a published book in her hand. The big wigs in the publishing world had accepted it. The introduction also mentioned the author had been working on the book for several years, after a painful divorce.

Jane realized that her idea wasn't only *not* original, but that Joan Jamison had been working on it since before Jane had even graduated college. Joe Frank did it in 1996. Angela Shelton's Documentary came out in 2004. In effect, Jane had stolen the idea, though the first time she heard of it was in a rejection e-mail. A big slap across the face. *Thanks again fate, you merciless bitch.*

Continuing, Jane felt compelled to wrap her head around all the story twists in Joan's novel, and if the idea intersected with her own book. *What book?* she thought. *It's dead. I'm on the last leg of a dead quest.*

She wondered if her friendship with Christian was really dead, too. No, she pushed that thought away. That was too much to bear while reading the book she had expected to write.

Worse than anything, the book was well written. It captivated her, and the pages flew as she consumed every sumptuous turn of phrase. As the story arc about the high school sweetheart unfurled, it wasn't hard to believe at all. It got Jane, and she found herself crying for the fictionalized version of the author who was rediscovering faith in love, in herself, in the world. On top of that, there was a layer of destiny and subtle allusions to classical literature.

The fictional Joan becomes convinced that God is working through modern technology to reconnect people and heal the world. It was just subtle enough that Jane swallowed the entire concept.

*Was everything a lie? All these other Jane Waldens, what the hell was that for? To teach me a lesson? Great. Got it Fate, thanks. But, did you have to take everything? I mean, what has it been, ten days on the road? Less than that? I hold this stupid book in my hand, this awesome, stunning beautiful book while I wait for my ridiculously delayed flight at La Guardia.*

*Okay, Fate – I'm over the cliff, my rope is frayed and I'm spent, and I'm sobbing, and I'm slipping. I have to know. Show me the connections. What was the actual link in the chain that started this?*

*Wait... oh yeah, it was that night. That night, and the liquor ice cream.*

*But that's just this trip. I must know it all. The origin, peel back the onion.*

Her flight finally began boarding. She got her things, all fully charged, and stood in line for the nearly five-hour flight to Biloxi. It was a cheap flight, so there was a stop, but she would not have to switch planes. She found her seat. She clutched *The Infinite Me.*

*Even the title is better than mine.* Then she thought, *Christian. I have to tell him.*

Jane felt numb. She should be a ball of sobs, scaring other passengers with her wild despair, but she felt empty. Nothing. It was all too much. How could it all go so badly, so completely, so fast? Of course, in some ways it felt excruciatingly slow. How many hours ago had she been in The Jane Hotel? How many hours, days, weeks did it seem since her life unraveled?

*Christian.*

Now that the book was gone, he was all Jane had left. But she didn't have him. That was over. Was it dead? The urge had almost overwhelmed her to call him, text him, find him. But they were telling the passengers to turn off their devices. Too late.

Images and feelings rolled through her. He wasn't even her type. Christian was no beefy, 80's movie star. The shallow though made her blush. Christian was right about one thing, her "type" hadn't made her happy – almost universally jerks. She thought of Christian's great hugs. His height was just right for hugging. He always put just the right pressure, his arms folded around her.

But what was he thinking when he hugged her? Every time he consoled her about a break-up, was he thinking, "Now's my chance?" Was he imagining them in bed, hugging in a very different way?

Every memory was tainted by uncertainty of intent. She though she knew him so well. *But that's the problem isn't it? Of course I love Christian, just not in that way. I'm even kind of honored that he loves me. But all that goodness – Christian, the best thing in my life - is poisoned by his silence. Was everything a lie?* She got out her journal. Jane had to get her thoughts down on paper, or they would strangle her mind.

The bombshell first: No book, and how much she enjoyed *The Infinite Me*, despite what it meant to her almost-writing-career. She recapped the emotional journey. To her dark mood were added two e-mail rejections in her inbox. They popped up as she typed. Both mentioned *The Infinite Me* as reasons for rejection. *You couldn't tell me this a little sooner?* she thought, then closed her e-mail and continued writing.

It wasn't long before it turned almost exclusively to Christian. She had to know. She had to explore every incident she could conjure, re-remember every event they shared, to finally know how he had deceived her. How long had his evil scheme been brewing?

*That first time we met. How old were we? 12, 13? No, 11. That's right, Christian just reminded me of this story. It was a birthday party for someone. Julie, I think. I wonder what happened to her. Are we* even friends on Facebook nowadays? Anyway, someone started the rumor that this kid liked me. I marched right over and asked him. *Do you like me?* I'd asked, right to his face. I meant to embarrass him. He was kind of cute, but he wore glasses and was kind of awkward looking, too tall for his age, all elbows.

The boy, Christian, didn't seem embarrassed at all. "You're pretty. But I don't want to be your boyfriend."

Young Jane was shocked by the bold statement, as were those few girls who hovered around the scene, in the corner of the backyard. She replied, "I'd never by your girlfriend anyway, Christian. Is that really your name? Sounds dumb."

"At least it's better than Plain Jane. Got any better burn than 'sounds dumb?' You can do better than that. How about, 'Your ears are so big, I bet you get free satellite TV.'"

Jane laughed at the jab at his own ears, which were large. She took up the challenge. "Okay. Your nose is so big…"

"Come on, you can do it…"

"Shut up. Your nose is so big people ski off it."

"Hey! Good one."

And that's how it started. Dumb kid's jokes, laughing together. Mocking each other. Mocking everything. Jane had nearly forgotten about that first day in the back yard. Especially the part about him not wanting to be her boyfriend. That had obviously changed.

But when?

Her hand flew as she documented the memories pouring out. Christian and Jane dancing with a group of friends at a ninth-grade dance, because no one asked Jane. When he found out, Christian and Jane learned how to dance from the internet. They spent hours in his room watching videos, doing terrible disco moves, whatever. They spent a lot of time in rooms. Classrooms, over at each other's houses, in bedrooms. Never anything romantic. But they laughed. Always that.

They ran the school newspaper together as co-editors. Then through high school, the group of friends melted away. A few moved away, others formed small groups, until, by college, it was just Christian and Jane, still working on a newspaper together. Always together.

Jane remembered the day she made Christian read her first short story. Well, it wasn't her first. She'd been writing since she was ten, but it was the first time that a story was good *enough*. Christian read the seven pages in her room. He laughed at spots, he got serious in others. When he was done, she saw a tear in his eye.

"I see a few punctuation issues, and a few sentence structure things. But Jane, it's good. It's really, really good. Strike that, it's great! You need to send this to someone."

He'd meant publication, of course, but Jane never did. Later, he threatened to send it in for her. He didn't. She remembered showing the same story to her sister, who never even finished it and gave it back only after being asked. Her mother read it and liked it. But, Christian had believed in her. Always. *But that's not how love works. I can't just turn on those kinds of feelings.*

Then in college, both going to the same school an hour away from their hometown, but living at home, she wrote her first story that she *did* submit. It was only to the college magazine, so only a handful of people ever read it. But she was published. That was the same year that Christian changed his major from Business to English. Jane hadn't noticed the timing of that before. It seemed especially important now.

Was he in love with her even then? He said he'd been in love with her since "forever." Why had he never said anything? The longer he waited, the more of a betrayal it became. All the boyfriends he hated. Sometimes he told her, sometimes not, but she always knew. Jane just hadn't understood why. Then, when she found them cheating with other girls – even in high school – she remembered the solace of the long weekends. Long days spent with Christian where he would occupy her time with things to take her mind off of those other, stupid boys.

Yet there he was, secretly one of those stupid boys pining away for her. *I was right there. What the hell was he waiting for?* She'd never felt anything romantic for him. She remembered Christian telling her that they'd kissed after a party. There was too much booze, so Jane had zero recollection of the incident. From then on, it was a running joke for a few years, simply referred to as the "incident." Christian would stop in mid-sentence, turn to her slowly and say, "Of course that was before... the incident." Jane assumed it was just another running joke between them.

If he'd been in love with her then, what must that kiss have done to him? He would never had taken advantage of her in that condition, of course. But what did it do to him emotionally? *Has my sub-conscience been teasing him? Trying to tell me something my conscious mind couldn't see?*

*And what was that thing he said about not being Jewish? Jacobson is a Jewish name, isn't it? I must have used that joke since freshman year in high school. I knew it wasn't that funny, but have I really been wrong all that time?* Jane tried to remember all the bullet points of their huge fight. She used her laptop to check the Jacobsen fact, and found to her dismay that Christian was right. *Has it really bothered him all this time?* Then she replayed the frequent quip in her head. It was always followed by Christian correcting her. She thought it was banter.

*Holy shit. Is Christian right? Have I really not seen him all along? Is he right that I need to open my eyes before I could even see his love for what it was? For what it is? Who had always been there for me? Only him. It was always him. Oh God, was it me that ruined everything?*

*No! No, wait a second here. He should have told me! I'm not a damn psychic!* But her mind was shifting. Rapid flashes of her life came to her. Every good time, every bad day, every life event, and Christian was standing right there. All the times they partied and ended up in bed together, or on a friend's couch. Fully clothed, of course, just friends. What torture must that have been for him?

She randomly thought of *Breakfast at Tiffany's*. At the end of the film, she lets the cat (named Cat) free, only to regret it and go searching for him. The movie ends with a happy Hollywood ending – she and Paul (whom she calls Fred the entire time) kiss and presumably end up together, Holly finally realizing that her best friend Paul is the one she loves. *My God, am I really living out my favorite story? Is Christian Paul, or the cat? Does it matter? Why the hell can I only relate through story constructs? Of course, in the novella it's pretty clear Paul/Fred is gay, so no happy romantic endings there...*

*What have I done? What is wrong with me?*

*The Infinite Me* was a blow. A terrible explosion, but this was worse. Her stomach had churned while reading the book, knowing it was better than anything she could currently write. But the realizations about Christian's true love rolled through her like mental landmines every place her imagination went. *But is his love for me enough? Even if I forgive him – of course I'll forgive him, if he ever forgives me – that doesn't mean I love him. Does it?*

Jane stopped writing. Her vision blurry from tears, she shut her notebook and sobbed in her skinny airplane seat, not caring whether it was freaking out the man next to her.

The pilot announced they were on the final approach. Devices must be put away. She automatically obeyed. The feeling of dread and loss flowed through her.

After landing, she disembarked, and realized in all the confusion, the life-altering last 24 hours, she'd forgotten to call Mississippi Jane. Jane called her when she was able to use her phone again, and was relieved to hear she was still welcome, even at this short notice.

*All these Janes. Was it just a waste? Vegas Jane with her career and family shit together, Mom Jane who is one of the only truly content people I know. How about Iron Jane. She's keeping her life together, while going through a slow-motion divorce. Is Christian right about Crazy Jane? Was I just looking at a mirror image of me? Is that what this whole trip was? Just shallow Jane meeting aspects of myself – who I want to be, who I'll never be, who I might be? Is that what I've been miss-ing?* She still wasn't sure. The one person she could ask, could probe the mystery with, was gone.

Checking to make sure she had enough cash for a cab, she was relieved for her secret stash. She hadn't touched it, since Christian paid for nearly everything. *Oh God, and he paid for the whole trip with his own money.*

Jane thought about arranging the ticket home be-fore leaving the airport, but decided she couldn't deal with it right now. She had to honor one last Jane, even if it was a fool's errand. *I'm the fool, alright.* Christian was in Texas by now, at least. She might still make it home before him, barring any 12-hour airport de-lays going forward. What did it matter? There was no hurry. No rush to write the book no one would ever publish. No hurry, since Christian might never forgive her. *I'm the one that freaked out and left. I left him in a strange city. You stood by me all these years, and I just left you.*

She wasn't sure she could forgive herself. For now, she did her best to push it aside. The cab told her how much it would be, and she figured she had enough for a round trip back to the airport. On the road, she got out her notes, trying to focus on a task instead of the various piles of messy emotions in her head, the dull weight on her heart. The questions felt hollow. Jane felt hollow as she headed to see her last Jane.

# Chapter 16

# Mississippi Jane

"The ending has to be inevitable, but surprising." –
Unknown

As Jane looked around Biloxi, Mississippi, she was
surprised by the number of concrete slabs. Many
were surrounded by lush green lawns that seemed
to lead nowhere. It was almost like they were the be-
ginnings of monuments. But they laid silent. Waiting
for what, Jane couldn't imagine. There were also a
surprising number of new buildings for such an his-
toric city.

Jane expected… well, she really didn't know what
to expect. She began to realize she should have done a
lot more research before she started this whole journey. It would have prevented all the mess that she
was now living through. She might even still have
Christian, if she'd paid more attention.

The cab pulled up to a small house, also new, by appearances. No more than ten years old, she would guesstimate. She paid, got a card from the cabbie so she could call for a ride later. She was hit again by how much the trip must have cost. *How much did Christian spend? That budget he showed me – what feels like a million years ago – did it really cost that much? More?* The guilt tugged at her. Jane suddenly feared for Christian's safety. The plan was to take turns driving back to California without stopping. She realized the fight had robbed them both of a good night's sleep. Now. he was barreling toward California, sleeping alone in his dad's car.

Jane had thought of calling, or at least texting a thousand times. Then the fear that he wouldn't answer. Then the fear that he would answer while driving, and get hurt. Mostly, she wanted to talk to him face to face. Anything else seemed hollow. She was done being hollow.

She knocked on the door and was met by a black woman about 60. "Hello there. You must be the other Jane Walden. Come on in."

Mississippi Jane had a Facebook page, but no profile picture. Our Jane wasn't surprised that she was a woman of color. "Thank you. It's very nice to meet you."

"Same here. It's such an exciting project that you're doing." Mississippi Jane asked, "How many Jane Waldens have you met so far?"

"It was supposed to be five, before you, but I got stood up in New York."

"*I'm* number five then? That's my lucky number! I always play the fifth slot machine at the new casino."

"Yeah. I was noticing a lot of new buildings. My vision of Biloxi was a lot more old south, or at least the 1950's era." Jane wanted to be careful. She had never met a southern black woman and was sensitive about certain subjects. "Oh, I hope that isn't inappropriate."

"No, no, not at all. I like blunt talk. Oh, excuse me. I've got some cookies in the oven. I'll be right back."

"Of course."

Mississippi Jane went to the kitchen, but spoke from the other room. "I know it seems cliché, an old woman baking cookies for her grandkids. But I've got five little ones that never seem to get enough." She came back in the room, "In fact, we should probably keep our voices down, I got one sleeping in the spare room."

"Sure. Sorry."

"You wouldn't even know that I was a successful lawyer before. But, I do make a mean peanut butter cookie."

"Smells like it," Our Jane agreed.

Mississippi Jane wiped her hands on her apron. "Well, Jane, how do we start?"

"Well, I have some questions, but I feel I need to be totally honest."

Mississippi Jane feigned seriousness, "Oh, well, then we better sit down for that."

They sat, Our Jane on the couch, facing the picture window, and the Mississippi Jane in a comfortable upholstered chair.

"I just found out that someone published a book very much like my idea. So, this interview may not ever see publication. In fact, I'll probably have to shelve the whole project. But I made a commitment to you, and I do want to hear about your life."

"I see," Mississippi Jane seemed genuinely concerned for Jane. It might have been Our Jane's own grandmother's voice speaking through this stranger. "I'm so sorry. That must be so disappointing."

"Devastating, yes."

"I'm gonna get you a cookie. You want some milk with that?"

Our Jane laughed softly. "Yes. That would be lovely."

Jane rose to look around the room and a picture caught her eye. It was a framed split shot photo, half the size of a poster. The top half showed some houses and buildings along the coast, labeled 1998. The bottom half was labeled 2005, the same area, but everything was gone. Wiped away.

Jane received her milk and two cookies on a paper napkin. She asked, "Sorry to pry, but what does this picture mean?"

Mississippi Jane said simply, "Oh, that's Katrina."

"The Hurricane that hit New Orleans?" Jane didn't want to eat during such a serious subject, but the delicious cookies were irresistible.

"The very one. What most folks don't know is that it didn't stop there. It hit Biloxi just as hard. Someone said that we 'caught the bad side of the storm.'"

244

Our Jane stared at the photo, "I had no idea. They only ever talked about New Orleans."

"Yep. Biloxi got overlooked at the time, but we were ravaged. A lot of folks said we were wiped off the map, and in some places, that was literally true. Everything was just gone." A special note of sadness crept into Mississippi Jane's voice, "We lost over 200 people to that storm, a lot more never came back to our city."

Our Jane put it all together. "That's why all the new buildings, the concrete slabs as I drove in."

"That's right. We have actually rebuilt quite a bit. In fact, for all the destruction, all the pain, Biloxi is stronger than ever. No one should have to live through something like that, but... most of us made it."

Jane took out her notebook, reluctantly. "Maybe you could just tell me your story."

Mississippi Jane thought for a minute. "Well, we southern ladies do like to tell stories. Got married back in '77. Jack was a good man. Jack and Jane. He was one of the people we lost in Katrina."

"Oh, I'm so sorry." said Jane.

"Thanks for that." Mississippi Jane smiled sadly. "He was a hero. Saved a little girl in the storm. Then he went under. Well, that was a long time ago. I spend the last years of my career helping Biloxi folks get square with all the insurance companies. I tell you, it was a mess. But eventually, most folks got paid right. My insurance company built me this new house. I don't think I could have lived on this spot without a fresh start. the old house had too many memories of Jack, you know."

Jane wanted to ask some questions, but didn't want to get in the way.

Mississippi Jane continued, "But now, I have the three grown kids, five grandkids. I spoil them rotten, then give them back to their parents for all the hell they put me through." Mississippi Jane laughed. "I had three daughters. I love them, of course. When they were teenagers, they drove me crazy. But all that fades when hard things happen. They made us stronger."

"Just like the old saying," Our Jane said. "can I ask why you keep a picture of the destruction. With your husband... I mean, doesn't it remind you..."

"Of course." said Mississippi Jane, still a smile on her lips, tinged with sadness. "When devastation rolls through your life. Well, we sweep so much away. We rebuild, and that's good. But we can't forget." granite entered her voice. "all those foundations you saw on your way here. Maybe someday they'll dig 'em up, build a new house there. I hope they don't. We should move forward, but never forget. This house is pretty new." She pointed to the picture. "But I have that to keep me grounded. A reminder of how bad it can get."

Jane thought of what talisman she would keep from her trip of destruction, the one that rolled through her life in the past ten days. *The Infinite Me? My plane ticket stub? That cheap plastic tourist crap I bought for my sister in New York?*

Our Jane looked at the picture on the wall and a wave of embarrassment rushed through her. "You've lived through so much, things I can't imagine. You let me into your home to chat about a silly project no one will see. And I'm realizing how selfish I am, because I still can't stop thinking about my Christian."

"My Christian?" Mississippi Jane perked up. "Many of us are Christian, especially after living through hard times."

"Of course. No, I meant my best friend Christian. A boy, a man named Christian. He's not a Christian... Oh crap, that's right, he probably is and I never knew it. Gosh, I'm babbling, sorry."

"It's okay, just get it out on your own time. We all have stories. Why don't you tell me yours, Miss Jane Walden."

"It's just... he paid for this trip, this foolish trip. Then we had a fight. A big, stupid fight. We both let it escalate. Me more than him, I'm sure. He said he loved me, you see. And I felt so betrayed, so lied to for all this time that I blew up... and then I left. I left my Christian. Then I found someone had written *my* book," Jane laughed, despite her bitter mood. "In fact, the very same night. Worse even than that, it's better than my book would have been. Which really sucks. But I don't even care about the book now, not really. I can't stop thinking about him."

"What does that tell you, then?"

Jane began to sob. Mississippi Jane went and sat beside her on the couch, grabbing the box of tissues from the coffee table. She didn't ask what was wrong. She simply rubbed Our Jane's shoulder until she trailed off naturally.

"And I'm sobbing over all these silly things in your house, a stranger, who fed me milk and cookies and is so nice. And you lost it all, and I'm whining about my silly non-problems. But he's still gone. I lost my Christian. I don't know what to do."

"Do you love this man?" Mississippi Jane smiled a comforting Grandma smile, and continued rubbing her back.

Jane wiped her eyes. She'd never really imagined it. *What is love? Isn't it exactly what I feel for Christian?* She answered simply, "I do. I really do."

The Janes hugged. Our Jane continued sobbing. She felt like she was embraced by her mother, her grandmother, every kind woman who had ever loved her.

"Then everything's going to be okay. I promise," confirmed Mississippi Jane.

Our Jane reached for another tissue, just as a car pulled into the driveway. It looked a lot like Christian's car. Another vehicle, this one an old truck, pulled up behind it. Her heart sank when it wasn't Christian who got out. She reminded herself that this wasn't a happy Hollywood ending.

"Oh, excuse me Jane. I have to see this gentleman," Mississippi Jane went to the door, and Our Jane rose instinctively with her. Since it was a small house she could hear the conversation at the door.

"Thank you, Paul. So nice of you to take care of it right away, and front door service, too. How much do I owe you?"

"Come on, Jane," Paul insisted, "It was just a flat tire. No charge. I don't forget all you did for me and mine. Here are the keys. You take care."

Our Jane was just behind the other Jane when she saw the keys. They were Christian's. They had the same San Francisco key fob she had bought for him.

"What... what's going on?" Our Jane was freshly bewildered. "Why do you have Christian's keys? His car?"

"The poor boy drove non-stop and broke down last night, not two miles from my house. Walked the rest of the way." She handed the keys to Jane, "You want to give these to him? I think it's safe to wake him up now."

"What? He's here? Where?" the words rushed out as she took the keys and spun around.

Mississippi Jane's warm laugh came out as she pointed to a closed door just down the hall. Our Jane rushed down the hallway, almost running into the door before the handle was completely turned.

Jane burst in, and Christian was under a handmade quilt on the bed. He was on his side, turned away from her. He didn't stir, even after the racket of the door slamming open. *He must have driven like crazy. He must be exhausted. How was he even sure I would come here, and not straight back to California?* She answered herself, *because he knows me.* How fateful was it that there were all those delays? She answered again, *because it is fate.* The Infinite Me *is right about that.*

She approached the bed slowly. He turned under the warm quilt, his eyes slowly opening as if he sensed her nearby. When he saw her, he bolted upright. She sat on the bed beside him.

"Jane! Jane, I'm so sorry. I shouldn't have kept my feelings from you. I don't know if you'll ever love me. I think I can live without that. I have all this time. But Jane…" Christian said breathlessly, in a rush, "Jane, I can't live without *you*. That would end me. Even if you never want to touch me, could never love me, I still want to be…

Jane's kiss interrupted him. It was long and deep, and passionate. She broke it long enough to reposition her arms around him and kissed him again. The kissing continued for a long time. There were tears from both; they were not from sadness.

Jane whispered, "*You* are my Gabriel Oak. You waited for me all this time."

She knew he hated that book, but he smiled anyway. Jane got serious. "But listen here, buddy boy. You can't ever underestimate me like that again. And I promise I'll never do that to you again. I remembered a phrase you used, and that's the only way it's going to work. Will you allow me to be your partner in love?"

He simply answered, "Yes."

Mississippi Jane stood at the door. "Sorry to interrupt. Jane, I'm guessing you haven't had a shower or much sleep in a while. Christian can show you where all that stuff is. I've got another guest room if you like."

"Actually, I just realized that except for a few hours in an airport chair, I am exhausted. But, could I stay here? I don't think I want to sleep without Christian ever again."

"Goodness, of course."

"It's not too weird, random strangers in your house?"

"No, no. What you don't know is that I'm a fine upstanding member of this community. Most call me Helper Jane. People stay over all the time, if they need a clean bed. When my grandkids aren't here, that is."

"Thank you." Christian smiled, Jane in his arms. "For everything."

"You're welcome. Feel free to stay the night. But don't thank me yet. I've got house rules – the biggest one is no hanky-panky in this house," Mississippi Jane smiled. "I'm an old-fashioned woman."

Jane tried to hide her disappointment, having just let feeling come to life that she didn't realize she had. "We'll be good. I promise."

"That's good. Besides, if I'm not getting any, no one else does either." They all laughed. Mississippi Jane finished, "I'm glad you found a happy ending… Well, it's a happy *beginning*, I suppose."

"Thanks, ma'am. Yes…" Jane hugged Christian tight, "Yes, it is."

# Chapter 17

# The Ashes

"Failure is the condiment that gives success its
flavor."
– Truman Capote

"I think quotes are very dangerous things" – Kate
Bush

Mississippi Jane left the door open to underscore her
no hanky-panky rule. Jane showered, alone, according to the house rules. She and Christian talked about
all that happened since they'd seen each other, which
was a lot. She pulled out *The Infinite Me*, but there
was no more time for tears. It was all laughter now. In
fact, they had to sensor themselves when the laughter got too loud. They laughed about their misadven-
tures for an hour before they fell asleep together, like
old married people.

Mississippi Jane insisted they eat a homemade country breakfast the next morning. There was grits, biscuits and gravy, country sausage, and all the coffee they could drink. No coffsugee here. Real country eating. Soon enough, they were stuffed.

"I couldn't eat another bite.," Our Jane said, holding her stomach. "Thank you so much."

"My pleasure," said Mississippi Jane. "Thank you for spicing up my weekend with this amazing story. Better than a romance novel."

"What do you mean?" asked Christian.

"Boy races across country for girl, girl falls for boy. Flat tires, New York City, fate, young love." Mississippi Jane sipped her coffee. "I'm honored to be part of your story."

"Maybe it will be a story, some day." Jane said as she looked deep into Christian's eyes.

Mississippi Jane noted the casual affection the two showed to each other. "Hold on to each other. Now that you found each other, don't let go. She'll make you mad, he'll infuriate you – because he's a man and they all get on our nerves sometimes. But let all that go. Don't even let a hurricane get between you."

Christian and Jane held hands. Our Jane thought of all that Mississippi Jane had gone through, the lives she touched, the community she built amidst tragedy. A tear rolled down her cheek. She promised, "We won't."

They finally said their goodbyes. The wonderful Mississippi Jane wouldn't take money, only accepting numerous "Thank yous" from both. They all hugged and left smiling. On the road, they made a plan about trading off to drive. It would be 30 hours, but they had no choice but to drive straight through. Jane had nearly maxed out her two credit cards, and Christian had just enough money left for gas and fast food.

They took as few pit stops as needed, giving themselves ample time to explore each other's mouths. They wanted each other desperately, but they kept talking each other out of a trip to the back seat. The Sebring's back seat in his dad's car was big enough. But it was, after all, his dad's car. The waiting was excruciating, especially the one-time Jane's left hand went exploring Christian's more delicate area, which almost caused several kinds of accidents. She refrained after that.

Fate smiled to herself. She thought of Jane's story and realized she was both the first Jane in many ways, and the seventh, since she'd changed so much. She liked this new version of Jane. Fate was happy to get Christian to Mississippi. He had tried to reprogram the GPS to go directly to California several times, but Fate refused to let that happen. She knew to keep him on course, how this story had to end.

The GPS happily announced, "Arriving at destination."

They made it home in 30 hours and 17 minutes, miraculously avoiding even one speeding ticket. They left their stuff in the car and ran for Christian's room in his dad's house. Luckily, his dad was at the office. They were too anxious to undress seductively.

They were both naked in a flash and in the shower together.

They took as much time as they could in the shower, washing and exploring each other's bodies for the first time. There was no talking. The shower was also a practical matter, having been on the road for so long, eating nothing but fast food. None of that mattered now that their hands and mouths explored.

Before long they were half dried and in bed. They tried to take their time, but the first time was over quickly for both; Jane though randomly of a literary analogy form *Lady Chatterley's Lover:* They both got to their own individual "crisis" quickly. Jane was pleasantly surprised at Christian's skill. Only having been with a few women before, he had obviously been paying attention.

The second time began fifteen minutes after the first. Jane took control, really examining Christian. Her mind threatened to compare him with Todd. She shut it down, and threw away that memory forever. She realized Christian had more muscles than she'd ever noticed, and in all the right places.

"You been working out?" she managed between breaths.

"I had to be ready, didn't I?"

They didn't sleep much that first night, or many nights after that. There was time for little else. At first, Jane couldn't figure out why it felt so different with Christian, so satisfying. She realized with a jolt. *It's because it's love. He's the one.* Jane moved in with Christian within a month, and they enjoyed long, wild nights filled with passion, and passionate days filled with laughter.

Between job hunting, Jane typed up the entire story and released it on her blog. She had been editing and filling out all the events from the trip. Christian was her biggest fan, and had lots of helpful suggestions about where to fill out, and where to cut.

Jane was home. She fit right into the Jacobson's cozy home. Dad often commented how nice it was to have a woman back in the house. The right woman.

The blog started to get picked up and followed by a lot of struggling and want-to-be writers. She did frequent guest blogging. Jane found a local writer's group and her writing improved exponentially.

Christian continued to work for his dad, of course. He and his dad decided that while they would honor the orders Christian made across country, they would expand throughout California first. Christian and his dad worked on a five-year plan together. They quite the Wine Guy and found another distributor that worked with them. They appeared on the menu of many local and regional restaurants. At the same time, the ABC Board of California had caught up with The Wine Guy. He was doing shady deals all over. His legal troubles would take years to unravel.

Jane finally found a job in a small accounting firm locally. It wasn't a dream job, but she liked her bosses, and the schedule left her time to write and be with Christian. Months after the trip, she got a message through her blog site. That led to a phone conversation. That night, when Christian walked in the door, she exploded with the news. "I talked to her: Norma Windell, the agent and editor with Busy Bee Literary. She wants to work with me!"

"That's awesome!" Christian knew Jane had been working hard on a few writing projects. "On what, exactly?"

"On the Plain Jane Blog! She thinks it would make a great book. She wants to work on it with me as an editor to start. But she really thinks she can sell it!"

Christian took Jane into one of his awesome hugs. The kiss was long, deep, and important. "You're awesome. I knew you'd be a real writer someday."

They'd been so busy, an old forgotten question popped into Jane's mind. "Hey, I never asked. You've told me everything, I know. But you switched to an English Lit major. Why, exactly?"

Christian smiled, like the last piece of a puzzle dropped into place. "It was for you. I read *The frogs Have It*. That amazing, funny, layered, literary story you wrote. Before, all your stuff was good, but after that story I knew I had to be ready to live with a writer the rest of my life. I had to be ready for you."

Jane kissed him, which led to a trip to bed. They had to use Jane's Queen size bed after they literally broke Christian's full size. It just wasn't made for the amount of love they were making. They had gotten quite good at it. After a long while, they were spent. Jane lay on Christian's chest.

Christian whispered, "You know we're going to have to talk about it."

"Hey," shushed Jane, "I told you things are too good. Let's not rock the boat."

"Okay. Okay. If all I have to settle for is hot crazy sex whenever I want it, and a beautiful, loving, talented girlfriend, I guess that will have to do." Christian paused, "Did I mention the sex is great?"

Jane arched an eyebrow. "I prefer show over tell."

"Nice! A literary joke and double entendre at the same time." Christian looked into her eyes. "If this is all I get, it's more than enough. You know you'll never getting rid of me."

"Ditto, mister." Jane stared back. "We didn't go through all that for nothing. No matter how hard you may want to dump me in the future. I am a handful, you know."

"You're at least two handfuls, but I can take it."

Jane smiled. "Can you? Because here I come again, kid."

Christian looked under the sheet, "Yep, looks like I'm all ready for you."

Before they got down to business, she whispered in his ear, "We'll go shopping for rings this weekend."

### THE END

Dear reader,
We hope you enjoyed reading *Seven Ways To Jane*.
Please take a moment to leave a review, even if it's a
short one. Your opinion is important to us.

Discover more books by M.J. Sewall at
https://www.nextchapter.pub/authors/mj-sewall-
fantasy-author-california

Want to know when one of our books is free or dis-
counted? Join the newsletter at
http://eepurl.com/bqqB3H

Best regards,
M.J. Sewall and the Next Chapter Team

# Author's Note

I love to travel. Don't you? I've been to a few other countries, 38 of the 50 states (Delaware and Maine, I'll get you some day!) and have driven across this amazing country four times. Many of the places in this novel are real, a few are modified, some made up, but of course all the states are real. I encourage you to visit them all. The Jane hotel in New York is real, Purgatory in Provincetown, Massachusetts is real. And many homes in that fun town do go for $1 Million, and more. If you end of visiting any of these places because of this book, feel free to contact me with pictures and stories. It's all about great stories, isn't it?

The original songs sung by the Sally Ann Trio in Wisconsin are real songs written by a friend of mine named Ryne Scott Paul Torres, and all permissions were happily granted.

This novel was inspired by my own ego-surfing. Turns out a lot of people have my name, as well. I thought of interviewing these other Mr.Sewalls, then realized they are probably as boring as I am. But wait! What if a fictional character did that very thing – and then the story became about more than I ever imagined when I started.

I hope you enjoyed the ride. I'd love for you to leave me an honest review on Amazon or Goodreads, or anywhere else you care to tell me that you liked the book. Or, just drop me a line anytime on my website mjsewall.com, or social media. I promise I won't be hard to find.

Cheers,
M J Sewall
January 2018

# Thanks and Acknowledgements

Special thanks to Mindy Conde and Natalie McDermott, editors extraordinaire.

Equally, I need to thank:

Anna Chastain
Brenda Artopoeus
Carol Weible
Danielle O'Brien
Hillary Frye
Janet Wallace
Jennifer Honey Moore
Judith Chumlea-Cohan
Nellie Sewall
Robert Lee
Rose Torres
Susan McCalister
Terri Jones

Seven Ways To Jane
ISBN: 978-4-86750-253-2 (Mass Market)

Published by
Next Chapter
1-60-20 Minami-Otsuka
170-0005 Toshima-Ku, Tokyo
+818035793528
8th June 2021

Lightning Source UK Ltd.
Milton Keynes UK
UKHW040906010721
386458UK00001B/152